D1237140
ACCA
13
TERRITORY INSPECTION DEPARTMENT
NATSUME ONO
H
ACCA
13

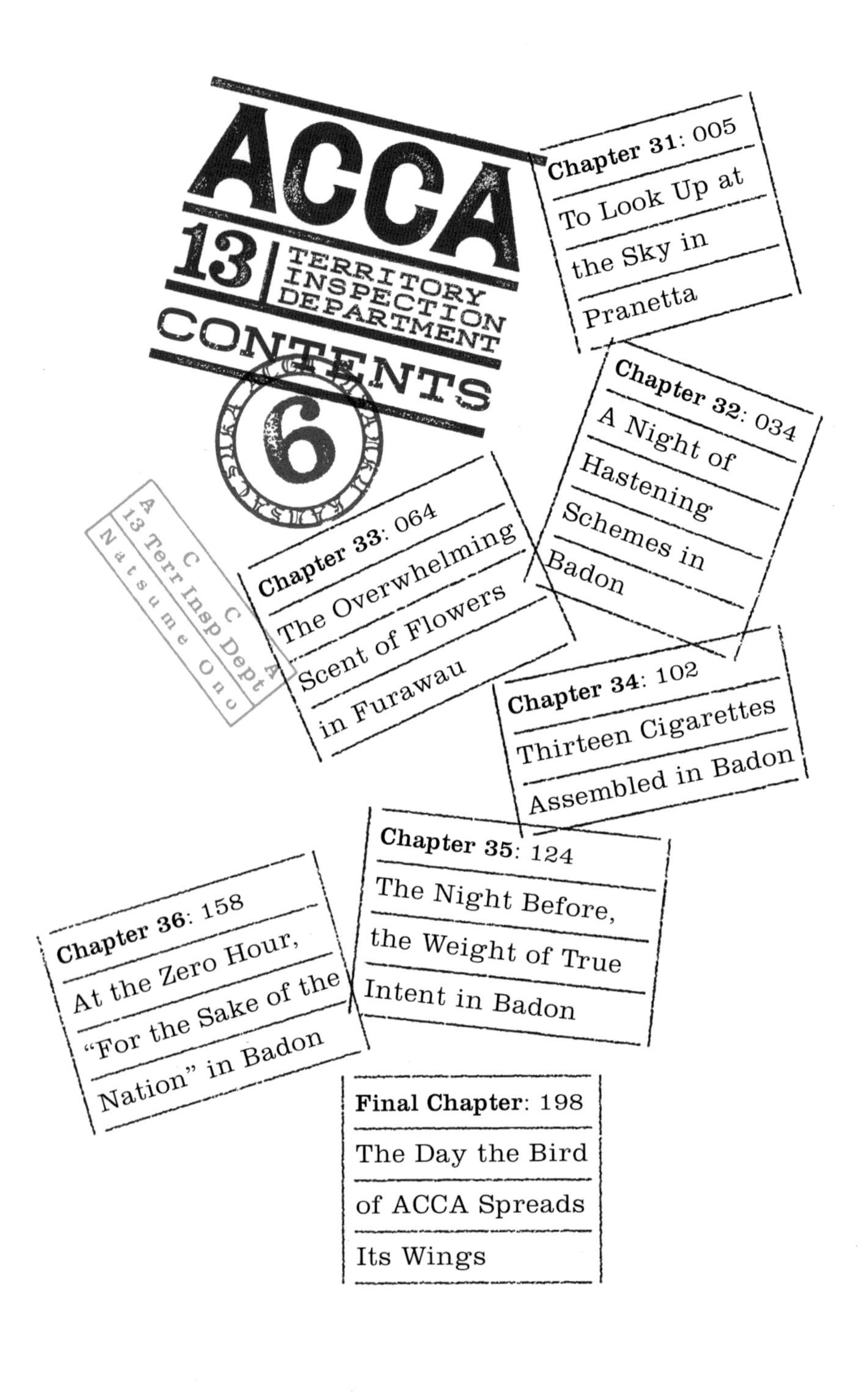
ACCA
13 TERRITORY INSPECTION DEPARTMENT
CONTENTS
6
ACCA
13 Terr Insp Dept
Natsume Ono

ACCA
13
TERRITORY
INSPECTION
DEPARTMENT
6
NATSUME ONO

ACCA
13

CHAPTER 31
To Look Up at the Sky in Pranetta

GOOD TO SEE YOU.
WE'LL BE HEADING OUT AGAIN THIS EVENING.
UNDER-STOOD.

HM? WE CAN GO FARTHER BY CAR NOW?
THE CITIZENS WIDENED THE ROAD.

IT'S ONLY US INSPECTION DEPARTMENT PERSONNEL AND THE DELIVERY SERVICES THAT DRIVE.
MIND YOU, THEY EXPANDED IT FOR THE DELIVERY TRUCKS...
...NOT FOR THE BENEFIT OF THE INSPECTION DEPARTMENT.
STILL, IT'S NOT AS THOUGH THEY'RE HOSTILE TOWARD US.
THEY TREAT US LIKE EVERYONE ELSE.
WELL, THAT'S GOOD.
MOST PEOPLE IN THIS DISTRICT ARE QUITE KINDHEARTED.

ANYONE WITH A QUICK TEMPER LEFT LONG AGO.

WE'LL DROP YOUR BAG OFF...
...AND THEN DO THE ROUNDS.
WHAT WOULD YOU LIKE TO SEE FIRST?
I SUPPOSE GOING IN ORDER IS BEST FOR THIS DISTRICT?
THEN CLOCKWISE FROM THE NORTH SECTOR.
MM.
THIS AREA'S THE MOST BEARABLE IN TERMS OF THE HEAT.
THE MAJORITY OF THE POPULACE ALSO LIVES IN THE NORTH SECTOR, SO THEY'LL LIKELY KEEP DEVELOPING THE AREA.

I HEARD YOU MADE THE NORTH SECTOR YOUR BASE IN YOUR LAST AUDIT AND THEN SPENT AN EXCESSIVE AMOUNT OF TIME COMMUTING.
THIS TIME, YOU'LL STAY IN EACH AREA AS YOU VISIT IT.
PRANETTA DISTRICT HALL
ACCA PRANETTA BRANCH OFFICE
THIS IS YOUR LODGING FOR TONIGHT.
THEY TAKE THE TOROCCO TRAIN TO THE MINE.
TOROCCO STOP
AND THEN THE MEN GO AND WORK IN THE SOUTH SECTOR, YES?
THAT'S RIGHT.
ACCA INSPECTION DEPARTMENT
......HERE?

I APOLOGIZE. I WASN'T ABLE TO GET A HOTEL.
IT'S OUR NIGHT DUTY OFFICE, SO IT'S STOCKED WITH ALL THE AMENITIES.
IS THERE A TOUR GROUP IN TOWN OR SOMETHING?

THEY'RE FILMING A SHOW.
HMM...
PRANETTA HAS FEW HOTELS TO BEGIN WITH, AND THEY'RE ALL FULL UP WITH TV PERSONNEL.
TV PERSONNEL ...?

...I THOUGHT HE WOULDN'T BE ABLE TO FOLLOW ME ALL THE WAY TO THIS DISTRICT...
....
...BUT HE'S PROBABLY WATCHING FROM SOME-WHERE...
VICE-CHAIRMAN!
IT'S NICE TO SEE YOU!
WELCOME!
THANKS.
I COLLECTED YESTERDAY'S REPORTS.
I'LL GO AND INPUT THE DATA.
THANK YOU.

SHALL WE GET GOING?
SURE.
I'LL CARRY THE WATER.
THANKS.

KAAAN (DONG)
KAAAN

TWO O'CLOCK?
THAT BELL'S QUITE HANDY.
IT'S EASY TO LOSE YOUR SENSE OF TIME HERE, YOU SEE.

THE LEVEL OF LIGHT STAYS THE SAME UNTIL EIGHT AT NIGHT.
IT IS QUITE DIFFERENT FROM LIVING UNDER THE SUN.

SOME PLACES IN THE RESIDENTIAL DISTRICT GET ACTUAL SUNLIGHT...
...BUT NOT MANY.

IT'S A DIFFICULT PLACE TO LIVE.
MM.

IT MIGHT BE A HARD LIFE...
...BUT EVERYONE LOOKS HAPPY.
ESPECIALLY IN THE EVENING WHEN THE MEN COME HOME FROM WORK...

WELL, THEY ARE CHASING A DREAM, AFTER ALL.

IS THAT A TV TOWER?

IT'D BE NICE IF ACCA COULD PUT UP AN ANTENNA HERE TOO.
THEN YOU COULD TRANSMIT WITHIN THE DISTRICT.
YOU WOULDN'T HAVE TO GO AROUND AND COLLECT THE REPORTS ON FOOT.

TV IS AN IMPORTANT FORM OF ENTER-TAINMENT FOR THE PEOPLE.
IT WOULD BE UNACCEPTABLE IF AN ACCA ANTENNA CAUSED RECEPTION ISSUES.

AND THIS WAY, WE CAN STAY IN SHAPE.
AGENT HARRIER BACK THERE PUT ON A LOT OF WEIGHT AT HIS PREVIOUS POSTING IN JUMOKU.
HE'S GOTTEN BACK TO HIS USUAL SIZE HERE.
BRANCH DIRECTOR!

I HEAR AGENT KORURI AT THE JUMOKU BRANCH HAS BEEN PACKING ON THE POUNDS TOO.
PLEASE DO SEND HIM HERE TO PRANETTA FOR HIS NEXT POSTING.
I'LL DISCUSS IT WITH THE CHAIRMAN.

HEY.
AGENT OTUS, THANKS FOR COMING ALL THIS WAY.
Director, Pranetta Branch
POLESTAR
WOULD YOU SEND THIS TO HQ FOR ME?
IT'S OUR RSVP FOR THE CELEBRATION.
UNDER-STOOD.
ONLY THE DISTRICT GOVERNOR AND I WILL ATTEND.
IN TRUTH, EACH DIVISION HEAD SHOULD ALSO BE GOING, BUT...
WITH A NUMBER OF US TOGETHER, OUR LACK OF UNIFORMS WILL DRAW UNDUE ATTENTION.

DISTRICT GOVERNOR.

ALL OF US HERE CHOSE NOT TO SPEND THE DISTRICT BUDGET ON UNIFORMS.
I DON'T REGRET THAT CHOICE.

IT'S JUST, WELL...
IT IS A LITTLE EMBARRASSING AS A LEADER.
District Governor, Pranetta Branch
ALTAIR

MAKES SENSE.
WE AGENTS ...
...DON'T WANT...
...TO PUT THE CITIZENS IN A POSITION WHERE PEOPLE WILL LOOK DOWN ON THEM.

ACCA-PRANETTA
NORTH SECTOR

FINISHED ALREADY?
MM.
NO ISSUES NOTED.

THIS DISTRICT RARELY HAS ANY MAJOR ISSUES.

THERE'S ALSO LITTLE TO REPORT, WHICH MAKES IT EASIER FOR US.
I EXPECT HE'S DONE WITH THE INPUT ALREADY.
I'LL GO OUT AND TRANSMIT.
I'LL COME ALONG.

SMELLS GOOD.
THEY'RE MAKING DINNER.
DO YOU HAVE DINNER PLANS?
WOULD YOU BE ALL RIGHT WITH JOINING US?

I WOULD, ACTUALLY.
REALLY?

I'M DONE WITH THE DATA.
I'VE GOT A REPORT FROM THE BRANCH DIRECTOR TO HQ. COULD YOU SEND THIS TOO?
ROGER.

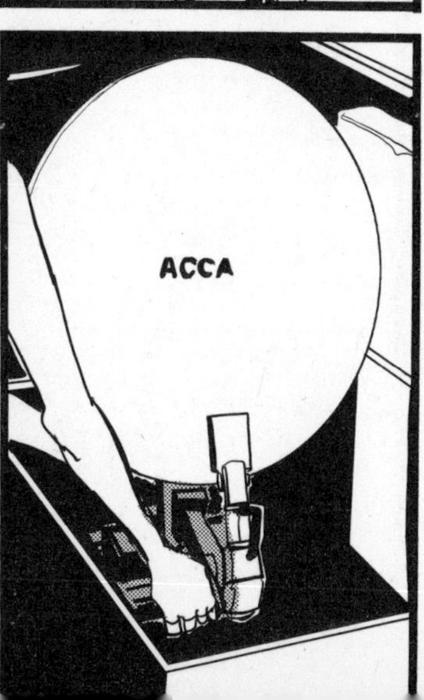
ACCA

ACCA

OKAY, WE'RE READY.

WE CAN'T SEND ANYTHING WITHOUT GOING OUT TO LOOK FOR A SIGNAL. IT'S A BIT OF A HASSLE.
BUT IT GIVES US A LITTLE BREAK, SO THERE'S THAT.
MM.
THE SIGNAL'S PRETTY BAD TODAY.
SHOULD I TRY ANOTHER ROUTE?
IT MIGHT BE BETTER IN THE EAST.
A STORM'S ON THE WAY...

GOOOOO (WHOOOSH)
...I CAN'T SEE A THING.
THAT'S THAT, THEN...
LOOKS LIKE IT'LL BE AT LEAST AN HOUR...
LET'S EAT.

WE ONLY HAVE EMERGENCY RATIONS, THOUGH.
DRIED BREAD
COCOA
BEEN A WHILE SINCE I HAD DRIED BREAD.
THIS ONE'S REALLY GOOD.
SO MANY DIFFERENT FLAVORS.
LEMON.
HUH.
...I'M STILL GOING WITH PEANUT BUTTER.
....
I'M SORRY DINNER TURNED OUT LIKE THIS.

THIS IS FINE.

YOU'RE ALWAYS THE SAME WHEN IT COMES TO WORK...
...BUT YOU'RE TOO CONCERNED ABOUT ME.
I'M JUST LIKE THE REST OF YOU.
BESIDES BEING YOUR BOSS, I MEAN...

?
WHAT ARE YOU TALKING ABOUT?
GOOD QUESTION.
HUH? IS IT A SECRET?
DRIED BREAD
THIS IS REALLY GOOD.
PLEASE TRY THE LEMON TOO.
CAN I OPEN THE PISTACHIO?
YOU DO LIKE NUTS, DON'T YOU, VICE-CHAIRMAN?
WE ALSO HAVE A TREAT TODAY!
JUMOKU POPCORN, CARAMEL AND CHEESE FLAVOR!
THEY SENT IT TO US THE OTHER DAY.
JUMOKU POP CORN
WE'RE NOT GOING TO BE ABLE TO FINISH THAT...
IT'S ALL RIGHT. I'LL POLISH IT OFF.
I WALK SO MUCH EVERY DAY, I NEVER GAIN WEIGHT.
LOCUSTELLA, PLEASE HAVE SOME.
...CARAMEL AND CHEESE, HUH...
THERE MIGHT BE TWO FLAVORS IN HERE, BUT WE CAN ONLY EAT ONE AT A TIME...
...AT THIS SIZE.
WHAT?
YOU CAN HOLD ON TO TWO, AT LEAST.
BITE ONE, THEN THE OTHER. IT'S THE BEST!
KU POP ORN

PRANETTA AND SUITSU ARE SAID TO BE THE HARDEST DISTRICTS TO LIVE IN.
BUT IT'S DIFFERENT HERE, COMPARED WITH SUITSU.
YOU STILL HAVE A FREE EXCHANGE OF PEOPLE AND GOODS FROM THE OUTSIDE.

...SUITSU HAS NOBLE AND PEASANT CLASSES...
...BUT THE DISTRICT ITSELF ISN'T IMPOVERISHED.
THE PROBLEM LIES WITH THE DISTRICT GOVERNMENT.

PRANETTA HAS THIS VAST EXPANSE OF LAND, BUT THEY CAN'T GROW ANYTHING. THEIR SELF-SUFFICIENCY IS LIMITED.
HERE, THE DISTRICT ITSELF IS POOR.
ACCA
THEY COULD USE THE RESOURCES PROVIDED BY THE CENTRAL GOVERNMENT TO MAKE THEIR TOWNS A BIT MORE LIVABLE, BUT...
...THE PEOPLE OF PRANETTA HAVE CHOSEN THEIR DREAMS OVER IMMEDIATE COMFORT.

AND THOSE DREAMS HAVE BEEN TIED UP IN UNDERGROUND MINING FOR MANY YEARS NOW.
THAT'S WHERE THE MAJORITY OF THE DISTRICT'S BUDGET GOES.

THEY HAVEN'T FOUND ANYTHING MAJOR YET...
...AND MAYBE THEY NEVER WILL.

BUT THEY NEVER GIVE UP.
NO RESIDENTS HERE HAVE ANY ISSUE WITH THE DISTRICT GOVERNMENT.
THAT'S WHERE THEY DIFFER FROM SUITSU.

THE ONLY REAL HARDSHIP OF LIFE UNDERGROUND HERE IS PROBABLY...

...THE FACT THAT THERE'S NO SKY.
THAT'S ALL.

I'M GLAD IT QUIETED DOWN SOONER THAN I THOUGHT IT WOULD.
WE CAN GET A MEAL IN TOWN.
I'M FULL...
HM?
THERE'S QUITE A CROWD OUTSIDE.
MAYBE THEY'RE FILMING THE TV SHOW.
NO.
THOSE ARE CITIZENS.
WELL, SOME TV PEOPLE ARE THERE TOO.
IT'S QUITE PLEASANT ABOVEGROUND AT THIS TIME. I ASSUME THEY'VE COME OUT FOR A LITTLE EVENING AIR.

IT'S ONLY NICE OUT FOR ABOUT AN HOUR.
IT'LL GET PRETTY CHILLY SOON ENOUGH.
THE TRANSMISSION GO THROUGH?
YES, SIR.
HOW ABOUT YOU JOIN US FOR A BIT OF AIR?
THAT SOUNDS NICE.
HAVE SOME LEMONADE.
THANKS.
DISTRICT GOVERNOR...
...EVERYONE FROM THE INSPECTION DEPARTMENT HAS RETURNED SAFELY.
THE STORM MUST'VE BEEN ROUGH.
YES.
THIS REGION REALLY IS INCREDIBLE.
THANKS FOR ALL THAT POPCORN!
WE HAD IT WITH EVERYONE AT SCHOOL!

I REALLY DO LOVE HOW THE PEOPLE HERE LOOK SO HAPPY.
YOU WOULDN'T HAPPEN TO HAVE ANY CIGARETTES, WOULD YOU?
D'YOU MIND?
OF COURSE NOT.
PLEASE, GO AHEAD.
....
WHETHER THE COUP D'ÉTAT SUCCEEDS OR FAILS...
...OUR LIFE HERE IS UNLIKELY TO CHANGE.

WITH NO REAL ROADS, IT'S NOT AS THOUGH WE COULD HAVE A LARGE HOSPITAL.
AND THE OCCASIONAL CRIMES WE GET ARE TRIVIAL ENOUGH FOR THE POLICE TO SOLVE AT THE SCENE.
JUST ABOUT THE ONLY THING THAT REQUIRES SECURITY IS THAT VEHICLE YOU ALL USE.

THE ONE PROBLEM WE'D HAVE WITHOUT ACCA IS THE MAIL WOULDN'T BE DELIVERED ANYMORE.
BUT I'M SURE WE COULD FIGURE OUT A WAY TO HANDLE THAT ON OUR OWN.
UNLIKE THE OTHER DISTRICTS, THERE'S NOTHING TO PROTECT HERE.
SO I DECIDED PRANETTA'D HAVE NOTHING TO DO WITH THE COUP...
?
I TOLD HER AS MUCH.
AND TO THAT, SHE SAID...

...WHEN WE DO FIND SOME CACHE OF RESOURCES AND THIS DISTRICT BECOMES WEALTHY...
...THERE MIGHT BE WAR.

ACCORDING TO HER, ORDER IN THIS LAND WOULD VANISH WITHOUT ACCA...

I TALK THE TALK ABOUT CHASING DREAMS AND ALL THAT...
...BUT I SUPPOSE I NEVER TRULY BELIEVED WE'D FIND ANYTHING.
MY THINKING NEVER MADE IT THAT FAR.

PRINCE SCHWAN WANTS TO ABOLISH ACCA...
...BUT YOU'RE ON ACCA'S SIDE. BETTER YOU ON THE THRONE.

THAT'S THE FUTURE THE COUP'S AIMING FOR, ISN'T IT?

IN WHICH CASE...

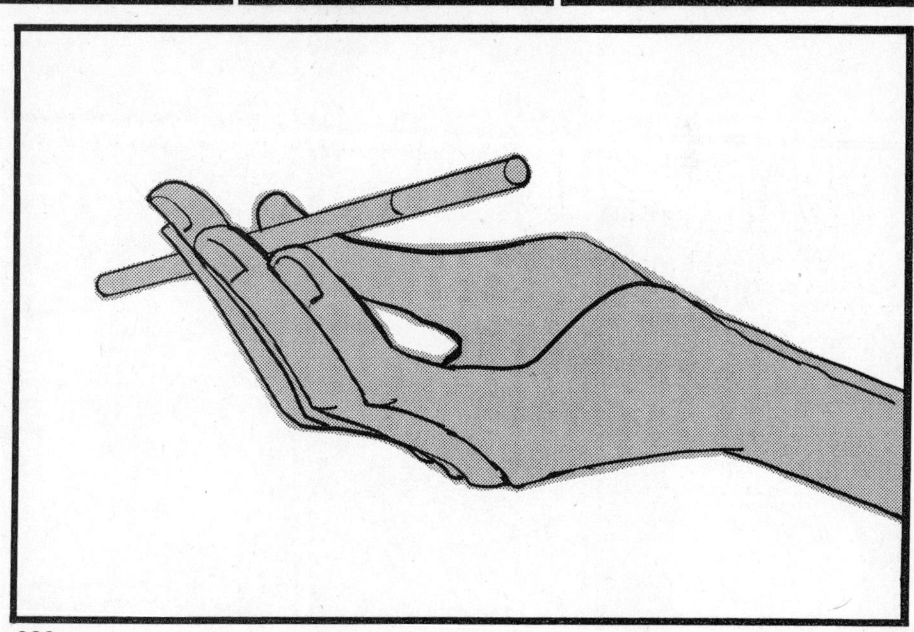

WE DON'T HAVE ANY POWER...
...BUT I'LL GIVE YOU THIS CIGARETTE ALL THE SAME...

HERE'S WHAT I THINK.

WHEN IT COMES TO PLACES FOR CHASING DREAMS, THE PEOPLE OF PRANETTA...
...ARE GAMBLING FOR MUCH HIGHER STAKES THAN ALL THOSE MEN IN YAKKARA, WOULDN'T YOU SAY?

I LIKE THE PEOPLE OF PRANETTA.
I SUPPOSE YOU WOULD.

I WISH THEIR LIVES ALLOWED THEM TO GAZE UP AT THE NIGHT SKY WHENEVER THEY WANTED...
...STILL LOOKING AS CHEERFUL AS THEY DO NOW.

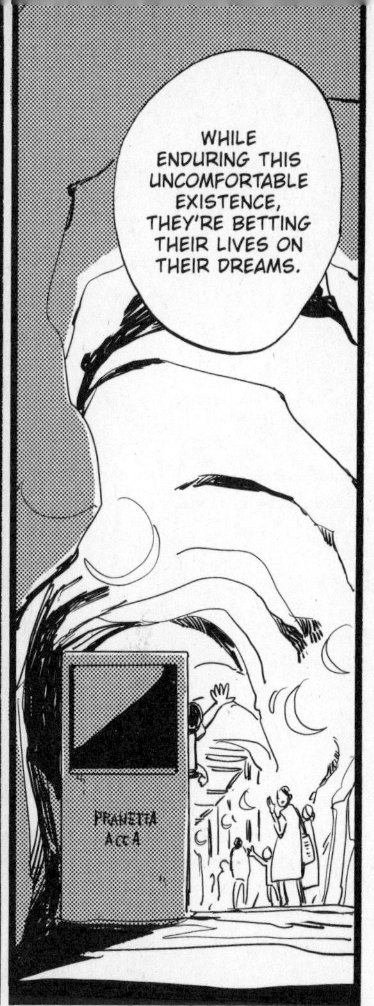
WHILE ENDURING THIS UNCOMFORTABLE EXISTENCE, THEY'RE BETTING THEIR LIVES ON THEIR DREAMS.
PRANETTA ACTA

VICE-CHAIRMAN...

WHAT DO YOU INTEND TO DO?

GOOD QUESTION.

ACCA Branch Uniforms | 12

Given the economic difficulties of Pranetta, government workers are not supplied uniforms, and the ACCA organization is no exception. An ACCA badge is sewn onto a shirt in place of a uniform.

CHAPTER 31
To Look Up at the Sky in Pranetta

CHAPTER 32

A Night of Hastening Schemes in Badon

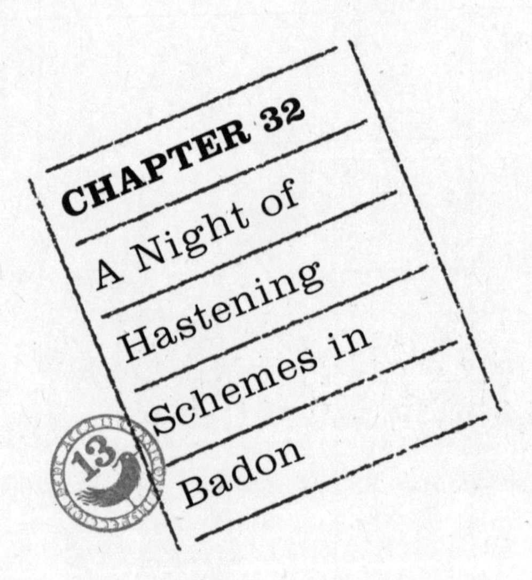

OOH! SO! MA! NY! PRESENTS!
THE CANDIES ARE SO SHINY!
CHOCOLATE DICE CAKES!
CUTE!
SUGAR?
SORRY. PRANETTA DOESN'T HAVE ANY FAMOUS SWEETS...
THAT'S JUST SUGAR...

I'M BACK.
GOOD TO SEE YOU, JEAN.
THANK YOU FOR SPENDING TIME WITH LOTTA...
...WHILE I WAS AWAY.
I DIDN'T DO ANYTHING SPECIAL. WE ALL SIMPLY MET UP EVERY DAY.
YOU CAN GET YOUR TRIP REPORTS TO ME SOMETIME THIS WEEK.
BUT CAN YOU SPARE ME A MINUTE NOW?
I KNOW YOU MUST BE TIRED.
I WANTED TO NARROW DOWN THE NEXT AGENT PLACEMENTS.

BADON
THIS WORKS, DOESN'T IT?
I THINK YOU'VE SORTED IT OUT QUITE NEATLY.
I DECIDED TO PROVISIONALLY ASSIGN PERSONNEL BASED ON YOUR REPORTS THUS FAR.

MOVING AGENT KORURI FROM JUMOKU TO PRANETTA... YOU'RE REALLY SOMETHING...
I HAVEN'T EVEN TOLD YOU ABOUT THAT YET.
HMM?

LET'S MAKE A FINAL DECISION ONCE THE AUDITS ARE COMPLETE.
WHEN ARE YOU OFF AGAIN?
THE DAY AFTER TOMORROW.
THAT SOON...
SORRY FOR SETTING IT UP LIKE THIS.
WE JUST HAVE TO FINISH BEFORE THE CENTENNIAL CELEBRATION...
IT'S FINE.
Korore
Suitsu
Dowa
Jumoku
IT SEEMS LIKE THE CELEBRATION WILL BE PRETTY EXTRAVAGANT.
MM.
HIS MAJESTY IS ALSO COMING FROM DOWA.
...OH, THAT REMINDS ME.
JEAN?
WHEN YOU GO HOME, MAKE TIME TO TALK TO LOTTA.

...ALTHOUGH PERHAPS YOU TWO ALREADY TALK PLENTY AND DON'T NEED ME TELLING YOU TO.
DID SOMETHING HAPPEN?

...A LITTLE INCIDENT WITH THE DOWA ROYAL FAMILY.

IT SEEMS SHE GOT DRAGGED INTO A BIT OF A KERFUFFLE.

LOOK AT ALL THIS!
THANKS!
THAT'S JUST SUGAR, THOUGH.
UH-HUH!

COULD YOU MAKE SOME TEA?
SURE!

IS HERBAL TEA ALL RIGHT?
WHATEVER YOU WANT'S FINE.

HERE YOU GO.
THANKS.

WHAT DO YOU WANT FOR DINNER?
HOW ABOUT WE GO OUT?
YOU DON'T MISS HOME COOKING?
MAKE SOME-THING FOR ME TOMOR-ROW.

WON'T YOU FILL ME IN ON EVERYTHING THAT HAPPENED WHILE I WAS GONE?

......OKAY.

MUGIMAKI

PLEASE TRY A SAMPLE.
MUCH APPRECI-ATED.

TAKE YOUR TIME.
...THANKS.

HE'S LEAVING FOR HIS NEXT AUDIT THE DAY AFTER TOMORROW.
...IF HE'S GOING TO BRING ME A REPORT, IT'LL BE TOMORROW, THEN...

KARAN (JANGLE)

GUESS HE WOULDN'T SHOW UP TODAY.

DIRECTOR GENERAL...
...HI.
WHAT A COINCIDENCE—
AAH, THE TRUTH IS I'VE BEEN UTTERLY BEWITCHED BY THE BREAD HERE.
HA HA HA!
PLEASE HAVE A SAMPLE.
WHY, THANK YOU.
I'D LIKE A THREE-CENTIMETER SLICE EACH OF THE WALNUT, THE MATCHA, AND THE BLACK SESAME.

DELICIOUS!
I'LL HAVE A SLICE OF THIS TOO.

IF YOU'RE NOT BUSY, HOW ABOUT A DRINK, DIRECTOR GENERAL?
HM?
THERE'S A FAIRLY DECENT STANDING WINE BAR RIGHT UP AHEAD.

I ONLY JUST RECENTLY DISCOVERED IT MYSELF.
IT'S A NICE PLACE. WE STOP BY THERE OURSELVES FROM TIME TO TIME.
OH-HOH! OF COURSE!

ALL RIGHT, THEN.
PI (BEEP) ピ
PI ピ
PI ピ
ピ
PI ピ
IT'S ME.
ARE YOU CLOSED THE USUAL DAYS THIS MONTH?
YES.
...UNDERSTOOD.
I'LL BE THERE RIGHT AWAY.

THAT DRINK WILL HAVE TO WAIT.
SOMETHING SERIOUS?
...IT IS.
I'M GOING TO HEAD-QUARTERS.

I'LL ACCOMPANY YOU.
WE CAN GET A TAXI AND BE THERE STRAIGHT AWAY.
PLEASE TAKE THESE.
FOR EVERYONE'S DINNER...
....
WE'LL TAKE EVERYTHING IN THE SHOP.
MAKE THE BILL OUT TO ACCA.
WHAT!?
ACCA COMMAND IS IN TOTAL CHAOS TONIGHT.

....
I SEE.

YOU MUST'VE BEEN SCARED.
I'M SORRY I COULDN'T BE HERE FOR YOU.

NO!
IT'S NOT YOUR FAULT, JEAN.
I MEAN, IT'S YOUR JOB.
...I'M GLAD YOU'RE OKAY.

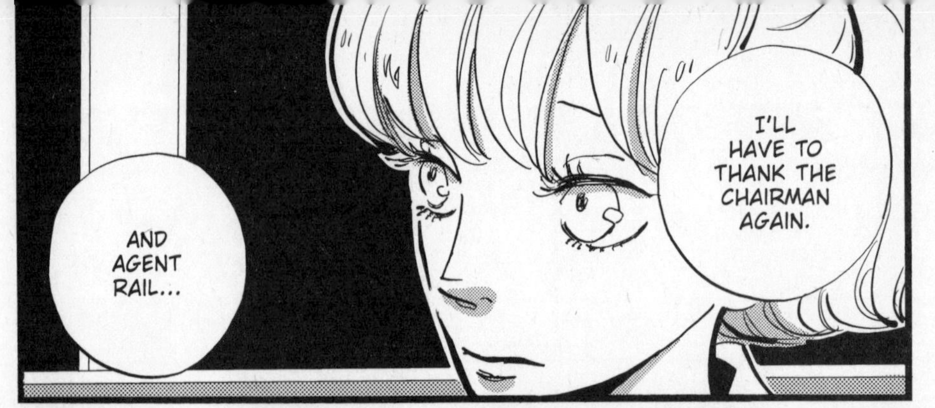
I'LL HAVE TO THANK THE CHAIRMAN AGAIN.
AND AGENT RAIL...

...JEAN.
WAS MOM ROYALTY...?

...THAT SEEMS TO BE THE CASE.

I JUST FOUND OUT TOO.

FROM NINO...

LOTTA.

NINO'S FROM DOWA.

HE SERVES THE ROYAL FAMILY.
HE'S BEEN WATCHING OVER US ALL THIS TIME ON THE ORDERS OF THE PRIVY COUNCIL CHAIR.

I ACTUALLY THOUGHT THERE WAS SOMETHING GOING ON WITH HIM.
...OH... YEAH?
I...
SEE, A LONG TIME AGO, OKAY?
I'M GONNA MARRY YOU, NINO!
I TOLD HIM THAT ONCE. IT REALLY WAS AGES AGO.

I WAS JUST A KID SAYING STUFF, BUT NINO...
HE GOT THIS SUPER-SERIOUS LOOK ON HIS FACE...
...AND HE STARED RIGHT AT ME AND SAID, "THAT'S NOT POSSIBLE."

THAT'S WHY I THOUGHT THERE HAD TO BE SOMETHING UP WITH HIM.
I WAS ONLY A KID, BUT I FELT IT EVEN THEN.

SO I'M NOT SURPRISED.

AND EVEN IF WE KNOW, THAT DOESN'T CHANGE OUR RELATIONSHIP WITH NINO, RIGHT?

...I'M NOT SO SURE ABOUT THAT.

LET'S GO EAT.
YOU'RE NOT CHANGING?
...I'LL GO GET READY.
NAH.
ピ
PI (BEEP)

We interrupt this program with an urgent news bulletin.

The Privy Council announced earlier that His Majesty the King collapsed...
...at the Dowa Art Institute awards today and was escorted out during the ceremony.

His Majesty was taken to Dowa Central Hospital and later returned to the palace.
But he remains in poor condition, and government affairs will be postponed to allow him to recuperate.

NO POINT IN US PANICKING.

THE BREAD'S ALL DIFFERENT COLORS, HM?
IT'S TRUE. ALL WE CAN DO IS WAIT FOR AN UPDATE ON HIS MAJESTY'S CONDITION.
ALTHOUGH I'VE NO OBJECTION TO BEING ON STANDBY HERE...
THE PLAN WE MUST EXECUTE BEFORE PRINCE SCHWAN ASCENDS THE THRONE...
WHAT WE URGENTLY NEED TO DISCUSS NOW, HOWEVER, IS WHAT COMES AFTER THAT.

I DISCUSSED THIS MATTER WITH CHIEF OFFICER GROSSULAR EARLIER.

...INDEED.

HE MIGHT JUST ABDICATE LIKE THIS.

WILL THAT IDIOT PRINCE FINALLY INHERIT ...?
OHH?
WEREN'T WE GOING TO HAVE A COUP BEFORE THAT?

BUT WE DON'T HAVE THE TIME AT ACCA EITHER.
BEFORE WE FUSS OVER THE PLAN...
...WE HAVE THE ACCA CENTENNIAL CELEBRATION TO CONSIDER.

VIPs FROM EVERY DISTRICT WILL BE JOINING US HERE.
WE CAN'T GO CHANGING IT UP NOW.
WE CAN ONLY PRAY THE KING'S ILLNESS IS NOT SERIOUS.

THE CELEBRA-TION...

WHAT IF WE COULD ACTUALLY USE IT?

HELLO THERE, CHIEF OFFICER GROSSU-LAR!
HM?
COULD I HAVE A MINUTE WITH DIRECTOR GENERAL MAUVE?
SIR!

I COULD HAVE COME TO YOU IF YOU'D JUST SENT FOR ME.
IT'S FINE.

YOU SPOKE TO OTUS, YES?

NO.
...I HAVEN'T MET WITH HIM YET.
DIDN'T YOU ORDER HIM TO REPORT ON THE STATE OF EVERY DISTRICT?
YES... HE DIDN'T COME TODAY.
HIS NEXT TRIP IS THE DAY AFTER TOMORROW.
IF HE DOESN'T COME TO SEE ME WITH AN UPDATE TOMORROW, I'LL MAKE AN EXCUSE TO CONTACT HIM.
THIS NEXT ONE WILL BE OTUS'S LAST AUDIT OF THE TERM.
HE'S GOING TO FURAWAU.

...I SEE.

WHAT REASON WOULD HE HAVE, DO YOU THINK...
...IF HE FAILED TO REPORT TO YOU TOMORROW?

I DON'T THINK HE'S FORGOTTEN.
HE MIGHT JUST BE BUSY...

...OR HE MIGHT HAVE SOME IDEA OR OTHER IN HIS HEAD.

I'LL AWAIT YOUR REPORT.
YES, SIR.

HOW IS MY FATHER?
DO THEY STILL NOT KNOW?
IF HE PASSES AWAY NOW, THEN...
...THE THRONE WILL BE SCHWAN'S...
DOWA
NO, IT'S NOT JUST SCHWAN.
SO LONG AS THEY HAVE QUALM'S AUTHORITY BEHIND THEM, SCHNEE'S CHILDREN IN BADON TOO...

TAKE CARE OF THEM AT THE VERY LEAST...
...ESPECIALLY THE SON WHO WAS ABSENT LAST TIME.
I WANT THEM CULLED. SEE IT DONE.
NO FURTHER FAILURES WILL BE TOLER-ATED.
KA (TAK)
KA
KA

WHERE ARE YOU GOING, YOUR HIGHNESS?
THE CHAPEL.
I WISH TO PRAY FOR MY GRANDFATHER.

I DON'T MIND HIM LEAVING ME THE THRONE AHEAD OF SCHEDULE...
...BUT I'D PREFER HE DID NOT PASS AWAY JUST YET.
WHAT A KIND HEART YOU HAVE, YOUR HIGHNESS...
GI (CREAK)
SO...
...MAKE SURE YOU TELL EVERYONE WHAT I JUST SAID.
BATAN (SLAM)
UNDERSTOOD.

MUGIMAKI

FURAWAU
DISTRICT HALL

IT'S A PLEASURE TO SEE YOU.

WELCOME TO FURAWAU.

CHAPTER 32
A Night of
Hastening
Schemes in
Badon
DEPT. ACCA 13 TERRITORY INSPECTION
PASS

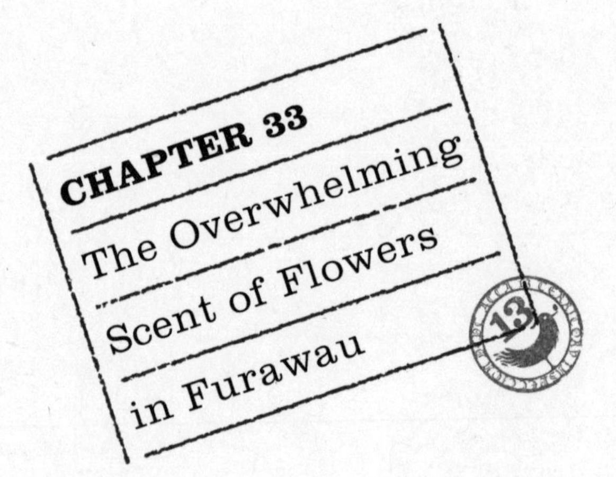
CHAPTER 33
The Overwhelming
Scent of Flowers
in Furawau
13

HAVING SOMEONE OF DOWA ROYAL BLOOD VISIT US LIKE THIS...
IT IS A GREAT DAY FOR THE HOUSE OF LILIUM.
ISN'T IT, BROTHER?
YES.
ERR... ARE YOU SURE ABOUT THIS?
I'M ACTUALLY HERE ON ACCA INSPECTION DEPARTMENT BUSINESS...

QUITE RIGHT.
WE ARE MEETING YOU IN OUR OFFICIAL CAPACITIES.
Director, Furawau Branch
YOUNGEST SON OF HOUSE LILIUM
PLEASE EXCUSE US.
District Governor, Furawau
OLDEST SON OF HOUSE LILIUM
WE MUST PRIORITIZE OUR DUTIES...
I SHALL HAVE TO CALL YOU "DISTRICT GOVERNOR."
YES, BRANCH DIRECTOR.
THAT'S NOT WHAT I MEANT...
HEH HEH.
YOU NEED TO TURN YOUR ATTENTION TO YOUR WORK, YES?

YES.
MY SUBORDINATE IS WAITING.
AT LEAST HAVE SOME TEA.
WE'LL SEE YOU OFF AFTERWARD.

IT'S AN HERBAL TEA MADE WITH THE BLOSSOMS OF FURAWAU.

THERE REALLY ARE SO MANY FLOWERS HERE. THEY'RE BEAUTIFUL.
THE PRIDE OF OUR DISTRICT.

ALTHOUGH FURAWAU IS THOUGHT OF AS NO MORE THAN A DISTRICT WITH UNDERGROUND RESOURCES...
...IT'S A BEAUTIFUL LAND FILLED WITH FLOWERS.
THE PEOPLE ARE THE SAME.
THE CITIZENS ARE AS BRIGHT AND ELEGANT AS THE FLORA.
THE FURAWAU DISTRICT REPRESENTATIVE'S QUITE KEEN AS WELL.
IS HE A RELATIVE?
HE'S A GOOD SUBORDINATE.

EVERY TIME HE RETURNS, HE SAYS THAT WHILE BADON IS LOVELY, THE SCENT OF FURAWAU'S FLOWERS SOOTHES HIS HEART.
YOU ALSO SEEM MORE RELAXED HERE THAN WHEN I'VE SEEN YOU IN BADON, GOVERNOR.
ALTHOUGH THAT'S ONLY EVER BEEN ON TV...

DOES CHIEF OFFICER LILIUM ALSO CHANGE WHEN HE RETURNS HOME?
MM.
I WONDER WITH THAT ONE.
MAYBE NOT.
HE IS FAR TOO SERIOUS, RIGHT DOWN TO HIS CORE.
HE'S THE ONLY ONE OF OUR BROTHERS AND SISTERS WHO'S DIFFERENT.
THAT AIR ABOUT HIM...
CHARGING STRAIGHT AHEAD...
HE SIMPLY THINKS ABOUT THIS COUNTRY MORE THAN ANYONE ELSE.

...THE CITIZENS REALLY DO LOOK BRIGHT AND SUNNY.
BUT IT DOESN'T FEEL LIKE CHEER...

...IT FEELS FORCED...

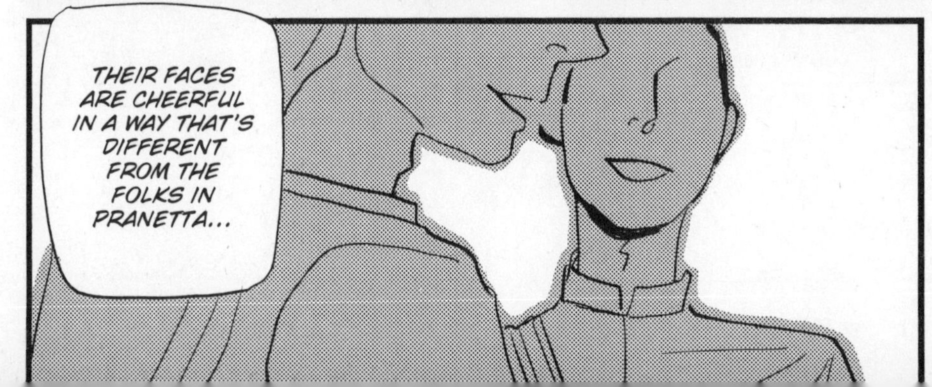
THEIR FACES ARE CHEERFUL IN A WAY THAT'S DIFFERENT FROM THE FOLKS IN PRANETTA...

ACCA
FURAWAU
WELCOME, SIR.
YOU MUST'VE BEEN WAITING. SORRY.
NOT AT ALL.
YOU'RE RIGHT ON SCHEDULE.
ACCA Inspection Dept.
Lead Supervisor,
Furawau Branch
CANARII

YOU BLEND RIGHT IN.
SORRY?
THE SMILING.
OH, VICE-CHAIRMAN!
I'VE ALWAYS BEEN A SMILER.

HMM.
NOT SURE HOW TO PUT IT...
IT'S LIKE YOU'RE COMFIER.
MAYBE?
AM I?

I SUPPOSE IT'S BECAUSE I LIVE SURROUNDED BY THESE FLOWERS NOW?
IT'S A VERY PEACEFUL FEELING.

....
THE CHAIRMAN HAS HIM GOING TO YAKKARA ON HIS NEXT PLACEMENT. I WONDER IF HE'LL BE OKAY...

HOW DID YOU WANT TO HANDLE THE AUDIT?
I'D LIKE TO GET THROUGH ONE TODAY.
VERY GOOD!
HOW ABOUT WE START IN THE SOUTH SECTOR? IT'S CLOSE.
VERY GOOD!

HOW DID YOU WANT TO TRAVEL?
...BY CAR.
VERY GOOD!
BY CAR.
FOR ALL THE SECTORS, THEN?
MM...
IS THERE ANY OTHER WAY?
A CAR IS THE MOST CONVE-NIENT.
......

AND THEN DINNER WITH YOU TONIGHT, I GUESS?
YOU HAVE AN INVITATION TO DINNER FROM THE DISTRICT GOVERNOR.
HE HAS ALSO ARRANGED FOR YOUR ACCOMMODATIONS.
ALL RIGHT. BUT LET'S MAKE SURE TO HAVE A DINNER AT SOME POINT.
HOW ABOUT WE ASK THE OTHERS? WE DON'T USUALLY GET THE CHANCE.
WHO SHALL I REACH OUT TO?
YOU'RE THE SUPERVISOR HERE. I LEAVE IT TO YOU.
UH...
....
....

...DID YOU ALWAYS WORK LIKE THIS?
UH...
THIS ISN'T THE FIRST TIME WE'VE TALKED, BUT YOU'RE ASKING QUESTIONS ABOUT EVERY LITTLE THING AND TAKING NOTES.
OH...
ALL OF THE DISTRICT SUPERVISORS ARE TALENTED, BUT YOU'VE ALWAYS GONE ABOVE AND BEYOND WITH A REAL ATTENTION TO DETAIL.

MY APOLOGIES...
...I REALIZE THIS ISN'T IDEAL, BUT...
WHAT'S WRONG?

...HERE IN FURAWAU, THE BRANCH DICTATES EVERYTHING...
...AND I GOT USED TO ACTING ACCORDINGLY.

...I FIND MYSELF WAITING TO BE INSTRUCTED RATHER THAN THINKING FOR MYSELF...
...I SEE.
I DO APOLOGIZE...
GU (SLUMP)
WELL, AS LONG AS YOU'VE NOTICED IT.
YOU ARE TALENTED, YOU KNOW.
PON (PAT)
...I'LL BE MORE CAREFUL ...!
YUP!
I'M TALENTED, SO I'LL BE FINE!
....

FURAWAU...

...REALLY IS SCARY.

OVER HERE.
...

I KNEW IT'D BE...
...MORE DIFFICULT TO MOVE AROUND IN FURAWAU THAN IN BADON.
I WONDER IF THE OTHERS ARE ALL RIGHT...
WHERE'S THE TARGET NOW?

DINNER AT THE GOVERNOR'S.
LOOKS LIKE HIS HOTEL'S IN THE CENTER OF TOWN, BUT HE MIGHT END UP STAYING OVER AT THE MANSION...
WE DON'T HAVE THE LUXURY OF GOING SOMEWHERE WITHOUT EYES LIKE THE OTHER DAY.
SOMEONE COULD COME ALONG AND INTERRUPT US AT ANY MOMENT.
WE HAVE TO MAKE SURE NOT TO MISS OUR CHANCE.
THERE'S NO ROOM FOR FAILURE NOW.

WHERE WERE YOU BEFORE THIS?
PRANETTA.
OHH.
RIGHT NEXT DOOR, HM?
EVEN IN FURAWAU...
...THE BORDER WITH PRANETTA IS A DESERT ZONE.
IT IS.
WHEN YOU GO OUT THAT FAR, THERE'S ABSOLUTELY NOTHING TO MINE.
BUT THE SCENERY'S TOTALLY DIFFERENT.

MOST LIKELY, THE WEALTH OF RESOURCES ARE CONCENTRATED HERE...
...IN THE SOUTHWEST OF FURAWAU AND AT THE BOTTOM OF THE OCEAN...
ALL I CAN DO IS OFFER MY SINCERE REGRETS TO THE PEOPLE OF PRANETTA.
I BELIEVE THEY UNDERSTAND THIS AS WELL, BUT...
...IF THEY'D USED THE RESOURCES ALLOCATED BY THE CENTRAL COUNCIL TO EACH DISTRICT...
...TO BUILD A CITY WHERE THEY COULD LIVE COMFORTABLY, PEOPLE WOULDN'T BE SAYING THE DISTRICT IS NOTHING BUT SAND NOW.
IS IT THEIR LEADER'S EGO?
NO.
IT SEEMS TO BE THE UNITED WILL OF THE PEOPLE.

IS IT, NOW?

HEH HEH.
NINETY PERCENT OF THE RESOURCES PROVIDED TO THE DISTRICTS ARE TAKEN FROM FURAWAU LAND.

IT IS OUR HOPE THAT...
...THEY BE EFFECTIVELY USED.

HERE IN FURAWAU, CITIZENS ARE ALSO UNITED IN A SINGLE DESIRE.
WHAT'S THAT?
PLEASE TAKE A GUESS.
HMM...

OUR PEOPLE ARE PROUD...
Kerore
Suitsu
Dowa
Yakkara
Pranetta
Furawau
...TO SUPPORT THE LAND OF DOWA.
OH MY! SO THERE'S ANOTHER THING TO BE PROUD OF.
WELL, OF COURSE.
THIS IS FURAWAU, AFTER ALL.

IF WE DO DISCOVER ANYTHING...
...WE'D OF COURSE LIKE TO SHARE IT WITH THE OTHER DISTRICTS.

BUT IT WOULD BE HARD FOR US IF OUR DISCOVERIES WERE SIMPLY TAKEN UNILATERALLY.
WE PROBABLY COULDN'T ACCEPT THAT.
FURAWAU HAS HAD RESOURCES SINCE BEFORE THE REIGN OF THE DOWA KINGDOM.
IN A WAY, THOSE RESOURCES HAVE BEEN TAKEN FROM THEM.
I WONDER IF THEY'RE ALL RIGHT WITH THAT...

NOW, THEN...
IT'S ABOUT TIME WE PRESENT IT, GOVERNOR.

ARE WE FINISHED DINING?
YES.
THEN LET'S MOVE TO ANOTHER ROOM.
WHAT DO YOU THINK?
I'M NOT VERY GOOD WITH WATER PIPES...
HEH HEH.

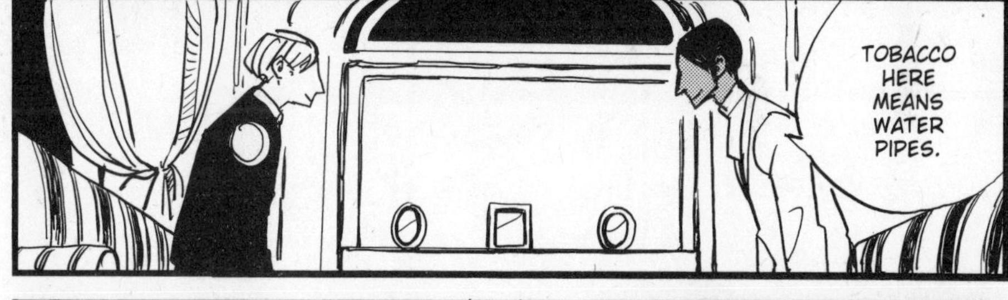
TOBACCO HERE MEANS WATER PIPES.

BUT TODAY, I'VE ARRANGED FOR SOMETHING ELSE.
A CIGARETTE.

FOR YOU.

YOU'LL BE ABLE TO, YES?

TO STAND TOGETHER WITH US.

IT'S THAT CAR.
HE'S BACK.
GOOD. I'M GLAD WE WERE WATCHING THIS PLACE.
...WE SHOULD JUST WATCH FOR A MINUTE FIRST...
NO, IF WE'RE DOING IT, IT HAS TO BE NOW.
LISTEN. WE AIM FOR WHEN HE GETS OUT OF THE CAR.

IF WE FAIL, WE'RE DEAD ANYWAY.
WE KILL HIM...
...AND BET ON SOMEHOW ESCAPING.

VICE-CHAIRMAN!

...THAT'S TROUBLE.
THE DRIVER TOO.
SO TOMORROW, THEN—

NO. SHOOT.
I DON'T CARE IF THERE'S COLLATERAL DAMAGE.
WE HAVE TO TAKE CARE OF THIS NOW.

JEAN!

ド
DON
(BLAM)
ド
DON

VICE-
CHAIRMAN
...!
NINO...

VICE-CHAIRMAN, PLEASE GET INSIDE.
TAKE THIS WOUNDED MAN TO THE HOSPITAL...
I MUST REPORT TO THE BRANCH DIRECTOR FIRST AND AWAIT INSTRUCTIONS—
THERE'S NO TIME FOR THAT!
IF YOU'RE WORRIED ABOUT GETTING IN TROUBLE, I'LL TAKE RESPONSIBILITY!
GUARDS, GO AFTER THE SHOOTER.
THE MAN ATTACKED IS FROM ACCA HEADQUARTERS.
THIS CAN'T BE COVERED UP WITHIN THE DISTRICT.
THIS IS AN OVERSIGHT ON FURAWAU'S PART.

...WHY?
YOU WERE THE ONE ATTACKED. YOU'RE FROM ACCA HQ...
SO WHY DOES EVERYTHING HAVE TO BE HANDLED INTERNALLY ...?

...NO WAY AROUND IT.
THAT'S THE FURAWAU DISTRICT GOVERNOR'S DECISION.
I'M SURE HE HAS HIS REASONS.
GUZU (SNIFFLE)
Unh...
Hngh!

...IF IT'S THE SAME PEOPLE WHO ATTACKED LOTTA...
...THE HOUSE OF DOWA HAS TO BE INVOLVED.
Uu!
Ngh!

...I'M GOING TO GO CHECK ON HIM.
YOU GO HOME AND REST.

THAT'S SOME BAD LUCK.

I HEAR THE SHOOTERS ARE DEAD.
THERE HAD TO BE MORE THAN JUST TWO. GUESS THEY GOT AWAY.
WHO KNOWS ...?
I'M NOT ALLOWED TO TOUCH THEM. I CAN'T LAY A HAND ON ANYONE FROM DOWA.
THAT'S WHY IT ENDED UP LIKE THIS.
FURAWAU IS PRICELESS.
THIS IS ACTUALLY MY FIRST TIME HERE.
FURAWAU'S THE ONLY PLACE I HAVEN'T GOTTEN INTO BEFORE.

MY "BOSS" FORBADE IT, YOU KNOW?
THIS IS THE ONLY PLACE WE CAN'T SMOOTH THINGS OVER SO EASILY.

BUT THIS TIME, I WAS ACTING AS CROW FROM ACCA UNDER THE ORDERS OF THE FIVE CHIEF OFFICERS.
I WAS ALLOWED TO MOVE FREELY THROUGH THE DISTRICT.
I'M SURE I'LL GET A PAT ON THE BACK FOR MY WORK HERE.

YOU'RE PRETTY CHATTY.
...I'VE BEEN WATCHING YOU THESE DAYS...
...BUT SOMETIMES, I DON'T KNOW IF YOU'RE BEING DRAGGED IN OR BUTTING IN.
...WELL, I WON'T SAY ANYTHING.
I'M JUST S'POSED TO WATCH.

JUST WATCH?

ENOUGH OF THIS, NINO.

YOUR LIFE DOESN'T BELONG TO THE HOUSE OF DOWA.

NEITHER LOTTA NOR I WANT THAT.

バタン
BATAN (SHUT)

JEAN.
I'M SO GLAD YOU'RE ALL RIGHT.

THE LEADER OF THE COUP D'ÉTAT...

...IS FURAWAU, ISN'T IT?

I WAS HOPING TO AVOID GETTING TANGLED UP IN ALL THIS BUSINESS WITH THE ROYAL FAMILY.
BUT I'VE BEEN DRAGGED INTO IT, WHETHER I LIKE IT OR NOT...SO WHY NOT DO WHAT NEEDS TO BE DONE?

THE PEOPLE DON'T WANT TO SEE...
...THE END OF ACCA.

I CAME TO ACCEPT...
...THE ITEM IN QUESTION.

PLEASE MEET WITH OUR BROTHER WHEN YOU RETURN TO BADON.

IT'S IMPORTANT TO ENVISAGE THE FUTURE OF THIS COUNTRY...
...AND LEAD EVERYONE TOGETHER.

HIS MAJESTY HAS TAKEN ILL.
WE HAVE TO HURRY.

ME? IN BADON?
NO THANKS.

WHY WOULD I GO THERE?
PUI (SNUB)
THE CEREMONY IS IMPORTANT, AND HIS MAJESTY WAS TO ATTEND. INSTEAD...
...YOU WILL ATTEND... AS THE NEXT KING?

......FINE. I'LL GO.
WHAT'S THE CEREMONY FOR?

TO COMMEMORATE ACCA'S CENTENNIAL.
I WILL NOT GO!

AND IF YOU MUST?
....

...ABSOLUTELY NO INTERVIEWS.
I'LL ATTEND THE CEREMONY AND RETURN HOME IMMEDIATELY AFTER.

YOU DO NOT WISH TO MEET YOUR COUSINS IN BADON?
I HAVE NO COUSINS OUTSIDE OF DOWA!
HE'S THE ONLY MALE CHILD.
ALL OF MY COUSINS ARE GIRLS!

SCHEDULE-WISE, WE MUST REACH BADON THE DAY BEFORE...
...SO DO LET ME KNOW IF YOU WISH TO MEET THEM.
....

MOST IMPORTANTLY, YOU WILL HAVE THE CHANCE TO ENJOY AUTHENTIC SANDWICH BREAD.

NO THANKS!

ACCA Branch Uniforms | 13

Furawau District

To avoid standing apart from the people, the traditional white garb worn by the citizens was adopted as is for the ACCA uniforms. ACCA agents or not, they still have pride in their own district.

CHAPTER 33

The Overwhelming Scent of Flowers in Furawau

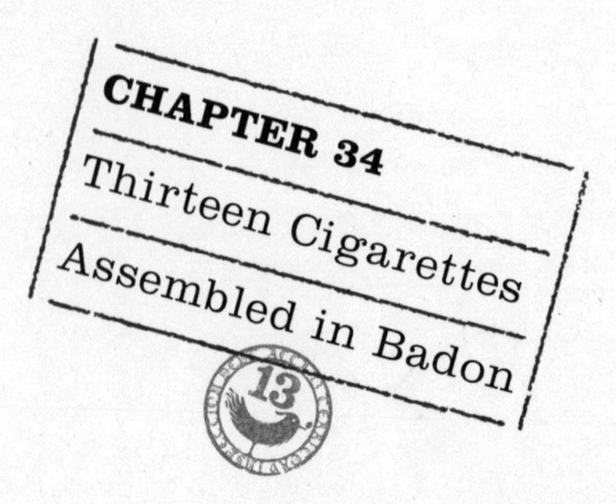

CHAPTER 34

Thirteen Cigarettes Assembled in Badon

CHESTNUT
MATCHA

I'M SO GLAD...

...YOU'VE MADE A DECISION.

CHIEF OFFICER GROSSULAR WAS ALSO DELIGHTED.

I HEARD CROW SAVED YOU.
HOW IS HE?
HE'LL STAY IN FURAWAU UNTIL HIS WOUNDS HEAL.
......IF HE WANTS TO, THAT IS.
I HAVEN'T YET BEEN NOTIFIED OF HIS DISAPPEARANCE FROM THE HOSPITAL...
...BUT IT LOOKS LIKE HE'LL BE BACK HERE SOON ENOUGH.
I'M TOLD HE DOES HAVE OTHER DUTIES, AFTER ALL.
I WON'T PRY INTO THAT, THOUGH.
THE DOWA FAMILY ARE SURPRISINGLY TENACIOUS...
...ESPECIALLY WHEN IT'S THE PRIVY CHAIR YOU'RE UP AGAINST.

ANYHOW...

...THIS IS OUR FUTURE.

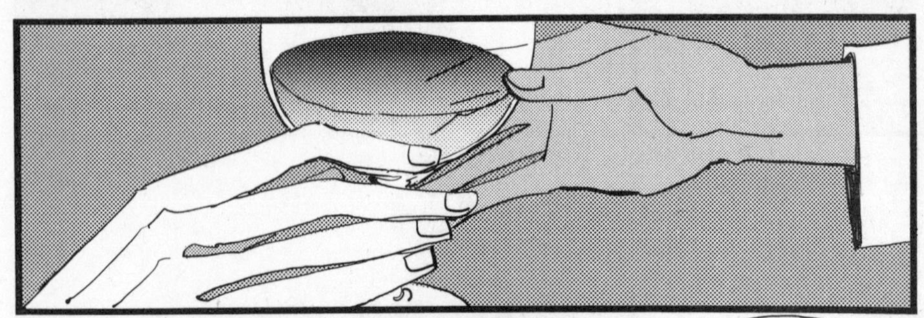

ONE WEEK UNTIL THE ACCA CENTENNIAL CELEBRATION.
IT'S UNCLEAR HOW MUCH CONTROL WE'LL BE ABLE TO TAKE THAT DAY...

...BUT WE'LL HAVE THE COOPERATION OF THE BADON BRANCH POLICE.
ACCA
NATURALLY, GIVEN THAT THEY PROTECT THE CAPITAL OF BADON, THEY ARE THE ONES TASKED WITH GUARDING THE CEREMONY.

HOWEVER, WE STILL DON'T KNOW HOW MANY GUARDS WILL ACCOMPANY THE PRINCE FROM DOWA ....

HOW MANY CIGARETTES HAVE YOU RECEIVED?

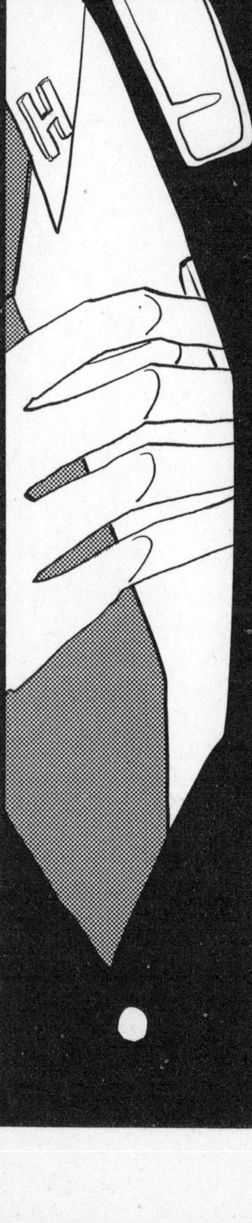

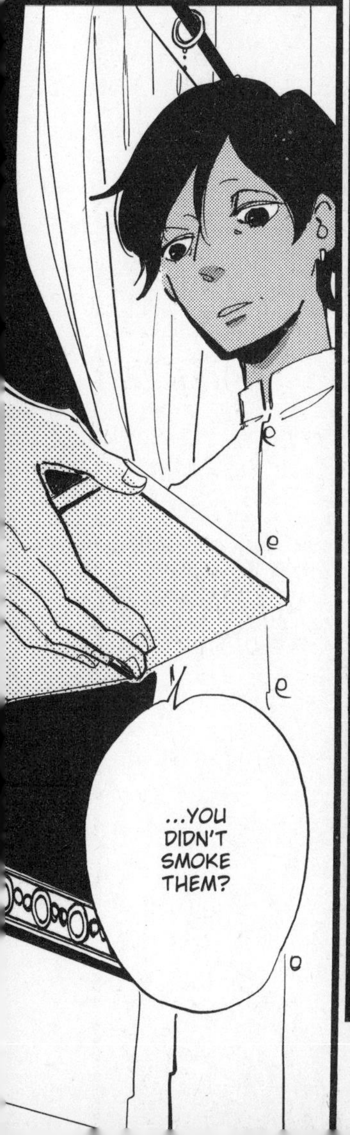
...YOU DIDN'T SMOKE THEM?

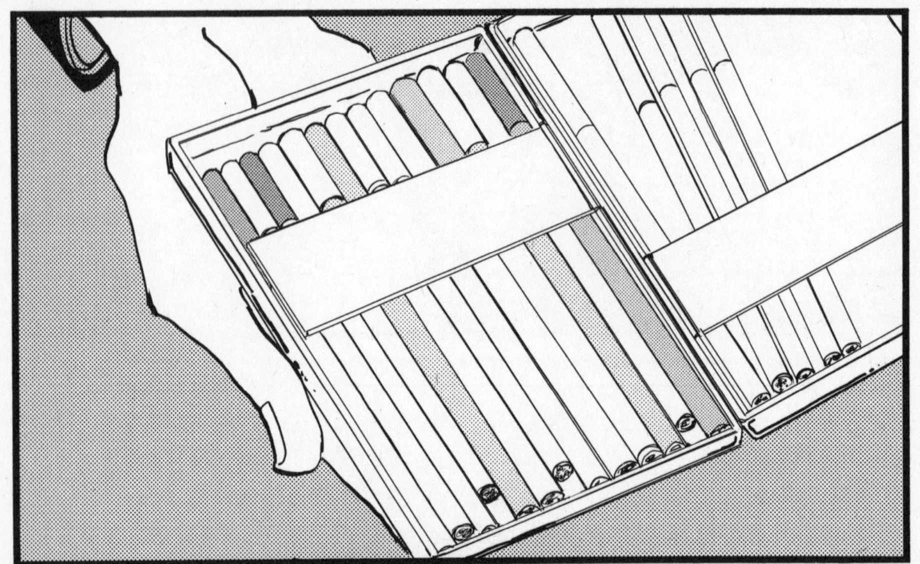

I WAS SCARED TO, SOMEHOW.
HA HA.

WE SPREAD THE WORD THAT DISTRICTS SHOULD SHOW THEIR INTENT TO TAKE PART IN THE COUP IN THE FORM OF A CIGARETTE TO THE "NEXT KING."

THIRTEEN...
EVEN DOWA.

LIKELY AT THE DISCRETION OF THE DOWA BRANCH DIRECTOR.
WE'LL FIND OUT WHEN THE DAY COMES...
I DON'T BELIEVE THE PRIVY COUNCIL CHAIR IS INVOLVED.
SO?
EVERYONE CLEARLY WANTS YOU—YOUR HIGHNESS TO TAKE THE THRONE.

IT DOESN'T HAVE TO BE ME...
...JUST SO LONG AS IT'S NOT THAT PRINCE.

BUT IT DOES HAVE TO BE YOU.
THERE'S ONLY YOU.
YOU'RE THE ONLY ONE WHO CAN PROTECT ACCA AND THE PEOPLE.

......WE'LL SUCCEED IN THE COUP...
...AND SET YOU ON THE THRONE.
THEN THE PEOPLE WILL BE ABLE TO LIVE AS THEY HAVE.

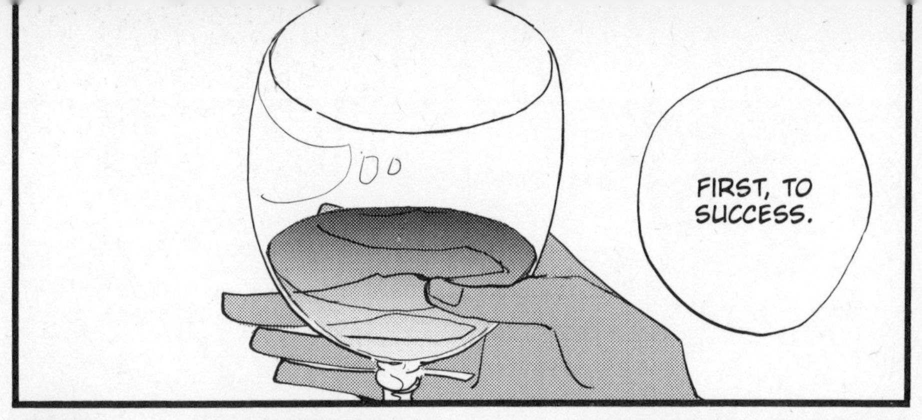
FIRST, TO SUCCESS.

DON'T FRET.
WE CAN WORK OUT THE DETAILS LATER.
YOU HAVE *US*.

NO NEED TO WORRY.

PIZZA
VICE-CHAIRMAN!
OVER HERE!

YOU MADE IT.

HERE, PRESENTS.
YAY!
I'LL MOVE OVER THERE.
GET IN, VICE-CHAIRMAN.
THANKS.
HOW WAS FURAWAU?

AGENT CANARII'S EYELIDS LOOK EVEN HEAVIER NOW.
KNOT CHEERED HIM UP.
I DON'T KNOW WHAT'S GOING ON, BUT CHEER UP?
DID SOME-THING HAPPEN?
NOTHING BIG.
BUT IT'S ALL RIGHT.
HE'S GOT A GOOD HEAD ON HIS SHOULDERS.
IT'S TRUE. I'VE NEVER SEEN AGENT CANARII LIKE THAT BEFORE.
MAYBE HE BROKE UP WITH HIS GIRL-FRIEND?
WELCOME BACK, JEAN.
RIGHT. THE SUPERVISORS ARE GONE FOR A LONG TIME, AFTER ALL.
IT'S HARD TO WAIT FOR YOUR BOY-FRIEND.
AGENT CANARII'S PRETTY POPULAR WITH THE LADIES AT HQ, RIGHT?
HE'S SO CUTE.
THE INSPECTION DEPARTMENT'S PRETTY POPULAR OVERALL, YOU KNOW?
THE AUDITS ARE FINALLY OVER.
FOR THE TIME BEING AT LEAST...
...THIS MIGHT BE THE END.

HEY!
DID YOU NOTICE AGENT RAIL OVER THERE?

OH, YOU'RE RIGHT.

MAYBE HE CAME TO SHOW OFF HIS UNIFORM.
HA HA HA!

...WHAT ARE YOU LOOKING AT!?
...SO YOU'RE BACK?

I WAS SURPRISED WHEN YOU ASKED, THOUGH.
COULD YOU KEEP AN EYE ON LOTTA WHILE I'M IN FURAWAU?
WHAT!?

NO BIG DEAL.

SORRY...
...ABOUT ASKING YOU TO WATCH OUT FOR LOTTA.

NOTHING HAPPENED HERE.
THANKS.
ACCA

...WHAT'RE YOU GONNA DO?

HM?
YOU'VE GOT ROYAL BLOOD, RIGHT?
ACCA

YOU'RE OLDER THAN THAT STUPID PRINCE.
COULDN'T YOU TAKE THE THRONE?

AND THEN WHAT?
I THINK THE KINGDOM WOULD BE BETTER OFF WITH YOU THAN THAT IDIOT.
HMM.

THEN MAYBE I WILL TAKE IT.
WHAT!?
YOU'RE GOING TO BE PRETTY BUSY, HUH?
EVERY OFFICER'S BEING MOBILIZED FOR THE CEREMONY.

IT'LL BE LIKE THE WHOLE CITY'S HAVING A PARTY, AFTER ALL.

VIPs are arriving here in Badon one after another from every district.
The ACCA centennial is this weekend.
In the Central Sector Hall Plaza...
KASHON (KACHIK)
I GUESS HIS MAJESTY WON'T BE HERE, THEN ...?

PRINCE SCHWAN'S COMING INSTEAD.

KASHAN

THE CERE-MONY...
REGULAR PEOPLE CAN COME WATCH TOO, RIGHT?

YOU'LL GET A BETTER VIEW ON TV.

07:38
...MAYBE I SHOULDN'T GO?

MM...

...JEAN...
YOU SEEM REALLY TENSE LATELY.

...I'M JUST TIRED.

CHAPTER 34
Thirteen Cigarettes
Assembled in Badon
DEPT. ACCA 13 TERRITORY INSPECTION
PASS

CHAPTER 35

The Night Before, the Weight of True Intent in Badon

Inspection Department

MORE LIKE YOU TOOK YOUR TIME BECAUSE YOU LIVE HERE...
...NO, AGENT GRUS?
COFFEE OR TEA?
....
SO WE'RE JUST MISSING...
...WARBLER, PARUS, AND EIDER?
Yakkara
Pranetta
Famasu
Furawau
Hare
WELL, HARE AND FAMASU ARE PRETTY FAR.
AND WARBLER'S GOT ALL THAT RED TAPE TO DEAL WITH.
AH!
YOU GREW OUT YOUR HAIR!
IT TAKES TIME TO GET OUT OF SUITSU.
YOU HAVE TO SIGN A BUNCH OF OATHS BEFORE THEY'LL LET YOU LEAVE.

IT'S BEEN AGES. IT'S PRETTY HOT HERE, HUH?
DUNLIN, YOU HAVEN'T CH—
WHO'S THAT!?
KORURI!? IT CAN'T BE!
IT'S QUITE LOUD IN HERE. SHALL WE TALK OVER THERE?
GOOD IDEA.

GOOD TO SEE YOU.
HELLO, EVERY-ONE!
PARUS...
...AND EIDER...
...TO-GETHER!
HYUUU (WHISTLE)
HELLO.
WE HAVE TEA FROM FURAWAU.

HEY, EIDER! JUST HANG ON A SEC!
WHAT IS IT?
C'MERE! OVER HERE!
YOU'RE AS COOL AS ALWAYS, AGENT FALCO.
KATA (CHK) KATA KATA
カタ カタ カタ
YOU TOO, AGENT KNOT.

SO, EIDER, ARE YOU IN LOVE WITH THE VICE-CHAIRMAN?
WHAT!?

N-NO—
IT'S OKAY. YOU DON'T HAVE TO HIDE IT FROM US.
YOU WERE ALL SHY WHEN YOU TALKED ABOUT HIM BEFORE.
YOU ASKED US IF WE THOUGHT HE WAS COOL.
HE ACTUALLY COOKED FOR ME!
SORRY!

...IT'S TRUE THAT BACK THEN...
...I DID, BUT...
MOJI (SQUIRM) MOJI
もじ もじ
...UM!
UM...
RIGHT NOW...
IT'S CUTE, ISN'T IT?
GIRLS LOVE TO TALK LOVE, HUH?

WHAT!?
YOU'RE DATING AGENT GRUS!?
OH MY!
ER...!
HE WAS REALLY THERE FOR ME...
...AND AFTER A WHILE, IT JUST...
YES...
KYAH!
BADON AND FAMASU! THAT'S SUPER-LONG-DISTANCE.
MM.
HE'S BETTER THAN THE VICE-CHAIRMAN.
QUITE THE SMOOTH OPERATOR, AGENT GRUS!
WELL...
...IT WOULD BE NICE IF WE ENDED UP A LITTLE CLOSER WITH OUR NEXT POSTINGS.

SPEAKING OF POSTINGS...
...ISN'T IT ABOUT TIME THE VICE-CHAIRMAN'S JOB OPENED UP?

HE'S ALWAYS PUTTING IN FOR A TRANSFER, RIGHT?
THE VICE-CHAIRMAN...
MAYBE THEY'LL FINALLY ACCEPT IT.

AND THEN WARBLER WILL BE PROMOTED TO VICE-CHAIRMAN.
PROBABLY...
AND SOME OF THE SUPERVISORS AMONG US WILL BE REMOVED FROM THEIR POSTS.
I'M TALKIN' DEMOTIONS.
WHAT'S WRONG?
ARE YOU OKAY ...?
.... YES...
FINE...
I'M FINE ...
AND SOME OF US'LL LIKELY BE POACHED BY OTHER DEPART-MENTS...
THERE'LL BE SOME CHANGE-UPS WITH THE SUPER-VISORS TOO.
AND THEN THERE'S THAT COUP D'ÉTAT...
DOKIRI (BADUM)
...HM?

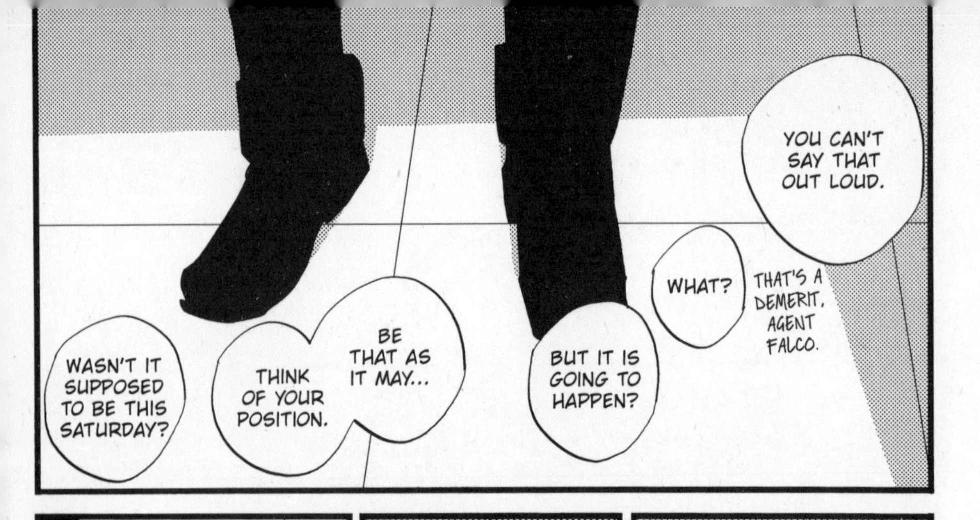
YOU CAN'T SAY THAT OUT LOUD.
THAT'S A DEMERIT, AGENT FALCO.
WHAT?
BUT IT IS GOING TO HAPPEN?
BE THAT AS IT MAY...
THINK OF YOUR POSITION.
WASN'T IT SUPPOSED TO BE THIS SATURDAY?

...WHAT ARE YOU TALKING ABOUT?
A COUP?
COME NOW!
SO, IN SUITSU-UUUU...
...YOU CAN'T USE THE NET, RIIIGHT? SO YOU DON'T GET MUCH INFORMATION, RIIIGHT?
ISN'T WARBLER REALLY READY TO BE VICE-CHAIRMAN?
THEN HOW ABOUT ME? I'M THE SMARTEST 'N' ALL!
I'D WORRY IF IT WAS YOU, PIPER.

IT'LL BE AGENT CANARII.
THERE'S... NO WAY...
WHAT'S WITH YOU?
WERE YOU ALWAYS LIKE THIS?
ARE YOU OKAY?
I'M FINE...
I'M FINE...
EVERYONE WHO GOES TO FURAWAU ENDS UP THAT WAY.
FURAWAU'S A SCARY PLACE.
I HOPE I GET YAKKARA NEEEEXT!
...KNOT.
WHAT'S THIS ABOUT A COUP?
I WANT BIRRA.
I WANT TO GO SKIING!
I WANT YAKKARA TOO.
ACCA'S TAKING THE LEAD TO AVOID CHAOS.
ACCA?
A COUP?
YES, ALL THE DISTRICTS ARE CON-SPIRING.
HANG ON A MINUTE... TO WHAT END?

TO SAVE ACCA... APPARENTLY.
GIVEN THAT PRINCE SCHWAN WILL DISBAND ACCA ONCE HE TAKES THE THRONE...
IF THE COUP SUCCEEDS, IT STOPS HIM FROM BECOMING KING.
AS LONG AS ACCA'S STILL HERE, THE CITIZENS WILL CONTINUE BEING ABLE TO LIVE IN PEACE.
THAT'S THE BASIC REASON AND PRETEXT.
AND HOW DID WE GET FROM THERE TO SOMETHING LIKE A COUP?
YOU DON'T THINK THAT'S WEIRD?

WARBLER.
YOU HAVE A MINUTE?

YOU'RE HERE, CHAIR-MAN!?
YES.
I AM.
MY DOOR WAS OPEN, YOU KNOW.

CLOSE THE DOOR, HM?

BATAN (SLAM)
CHAIR-MAN...
THIS MATTER WAS DECIDED BY OUR SUPERIORS...

...THE FIVE CHIEF OFFICERS AND THE DIRECTOR GENERAL...

...BASED ON THE THINKING THAT IF A COUP IS INEVITABLE...
...THEN ACCA SHOULD TAKE THE LEAD TO PREVENT TOTAL CHAOS.

INEVITABLE?
IMPOSSIBLE.
NO MATTER HOW DISSATISFIED THE DISTRICTS ARE, THEY GAIN SO MUCH MORE FROM BEING UNIFIED.

WE DON'T KNOW IF ACCA WILL ACTUALLY BE DISBANDED...
PERHAPS THE PRINCE IS JUST TALK?

HE MIGHT BE A FOOL, BUT WOULD HE HONESTLY BE A DICTATOR?
ABOUT ALL HE'S CAPABLE OF DOING IS WHATEVER THE PRIVY COUNCIL SAYS.

DOWA KNOWS THE EXTENT OF THEIR POWER.
AFTER ALL THIS TIME, THEY WOULDN'T FORCE A DESPOTIC RULE OR DO ANYTHING TO RUIN THE WAY THINGS ARE NOW.
I DON'T BELIEVE THE PRETEXT OF "SAVING ACCA" WILL HONESTLY FLY.

YOU CAN'T SAY WITH CERTAINTY THAT ACCA WILL SURVIVE.
AND THERE IS NOTHING MORE FRIGHTENING THAN A FOOL.
A FOOL IS HAPPY TO TIE A NOOSE AROUND HIS OWN NECK.
ACCA MUST INDEED NOT BE DISBANDED.
THAT IS WHAT THE PEOPLE OF THIS COUNTRY WANT.
...YOU'RE TOO FOCUSED ON ACCA.
YOU'RE ALL MAD...

RECENTLY...
...IT SEEMS YOU HAVEN'T BEEN GOING TO BUY BREAD.

...THAT'S TRUE.

...IT APPEARS THAT THE CIGARETTES I'VE BEEN GIVEN FROM EACH DISTRICT...
...ARE A SHOW OF THEIR INTENT TO PARTICIPATE IN THE COUP.
I HEAR YOU HAVE... A TOTAL OF THIRTEEN.
THE FIVE CHIEF OFFICERS INFORMED ME.
...IT WAS I WHO INFORMED CHIEF OFFICER LILIUM.

SO YOU MET WITH CHIEF OFFICER LILIUM BEFORE ME?
HMM.

...AND WHAT ORDERS DID HE GIVE YOU?

......NOT SO MUCH ORDERS AS...

UNDER-STOOD.

FURTHER REPORTS WILL NOT BE REQUIRED.

....
THEN IF YOU'LL EXCUSE ME...

OTUS.

YOU'RE ALL RIGHT?

YES.

WHY WOULD THE DIRECTOR GENERAL CALL OTUS IN...?
THEY'RE PROBABLY TALKING ABOUT THE BAKERY...
WARBLER.

LOCUSTELLA TOLD ME.
HE'S QUITE OUT OF THE LOOP IN SUITSU...
...SO I TOOK IT UPON MYSELF TO INFORM HIM.

...YOU MEAN ABOUT MY HERITAGE?
YOU'RE PROBABLY THE ONLY ONE OF THE SUPERVISORS WHO KNOWS...
...LOCUS-TELLA.
WHAT?
......THE COUP SUPPORTERS...

...NO.
THE WHOLE OF ACCA IS THE INSTIGATOR OF THIS COUP.
THEY INTEND TO SET YOU UP AS THE NEXT KING, IS THAT IT?

IF WE MUST PICK BETWEEN THE KING'S GRANDSONS, THEN YOU WOULD INDEED BE WELCOMED OVER THE UNPOPULAR PRINCE SCHWAN.
YOU MIGHT BE A DARK HORSE, BUT YOU'RE WITH ACCA, THE PRIDE OF THE CITIZENS.

IF THE PRIVY CHAIR ALSO PREFERS YOU...
...THEN THERE'S NO PROBLEM.
HE'LL LIKELY ACCEPT THE COUP.

...YOU WENT TO THE DIRECTOR GENERAL'S OFFICE?

SO YOU'RE ON BOARD, THEN.

YOU'VE GOT NO INTEREST IN THE THRONE, HAVE YOU?
IS THIS FOR ACCA'S SAKE?

...ISN'T THAT A BIT FOOLISH?

...I REALLY DO WANT YOU TO TAKE MY JOB AFTER I LEAVE.

BUT MAYBE HANG ON A LITTLE LONGER.

THAT PRINCE...
...SURE IS A HANDFUL, HM?

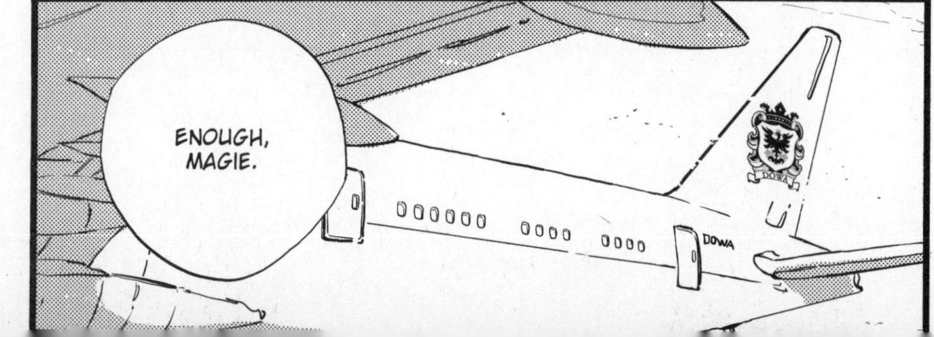
ENOUGH, MAGIE.
DOWA

I TOLD YOU I WOULDN'T SEE THEM.
THESE COUSINS OR WHAT HAVE YOU ...
PUI (FWIP)
...SO...
...MY AUNT SENT HER MEN, BUT THE GIRL IS ALL RIGHT.
HMPH!
WHAT IS SHE—
NO MATTER!
PUN (FUME)
WHETHER SHE LIVES OR DIES...
...HAS GOT NOTHING TO DO WITH ME.

...YOUR HIGHNESS.

PERHAPS YOU SHOULD TAKE A LITTLE MORE INTEREST IN THE PEOPLE...IN THE COUNTRY.
AT LEAST TRY TO BE WELL-LIKED AMONG YOUR RELATIVES.
HMPH!
IF THEY WANT TO STAY AWAY, THEN LET THEM!
THEY'RE HARDLY ANY USE TO ME ANYWAY!
ARE YOU SAYING THEY HATE ME?
....
....

I'M NOT TALKING ABOUT YOU ALL!
...I UNDER-STAND.
IT'S FINE.
...I AM THE KING OF DOWA.

VIPs from every district have already descended on Badon.
And earlier, Prince Schwan arrived from Dowa.

His Highness proceeded to his hotel...
WHAT? MAGIE?
SO HE'S IN THE DOWA FAMILY ROYAL GUARD...!?

The ACCA centennial ceremony is tomorrow...
THAT'S THE PERSON I MET AT THE BREAD SHOP...

I GUESS THAT'S THE FRIEND IN DOWA AGENT RAIL MENTIONED...
...SO THEN...

TONIGHT IS THE FINAL MEETING WITH THE REPRESENTATIVES FROM EACH DISTRICT.

THIS IS WHAT THE HOUSE OF LILIUM HAS BEEN WAITING FOR.

...TOMORROW, AT LONG LAST...
I CAN SEE A DAZZLING FUTURE AHEAD.

THE COUP WILL SUCCEED...
...AND OTUS WILL GAIN THE RIGHT TO BE THE NEXT KING.

YOU SAID THE HOUSE OF LILIUM, YES?

YOU'VE ALSO BEEN WAITING.
EVERYONE HAS.
AM I WRONG?
ENOUGH.

...SAY WHAT YOU REALLY MEAN.

...I DID.

PUT OTUS UP THERE.

CONTROL OTUS.
CONTROL THE COUNTRY.

BY THE TIME ANYONE NOTICES, THEY'LL HAVE NO CHOICE...
...BUT TO ACCEPT FURAWAU AS THE REAL POWER IN THIS LAND.

WHEN THEY DO REALIZE, IT WILL BE TOO LATE.
JUST LIKE IT IS FOR YOU NOW...

SOME PART OF YOU HAD TO HAVE KNOWN...
...THAT THINGS COULDN'T GO ON LIKE THIS, SO WHY DIDN'T YOU RESIST?
IT'S BECAUSE YOU WERE UP AGAINST...
...HOUSE LILIUM OF THE NATION OF FURAWAU.

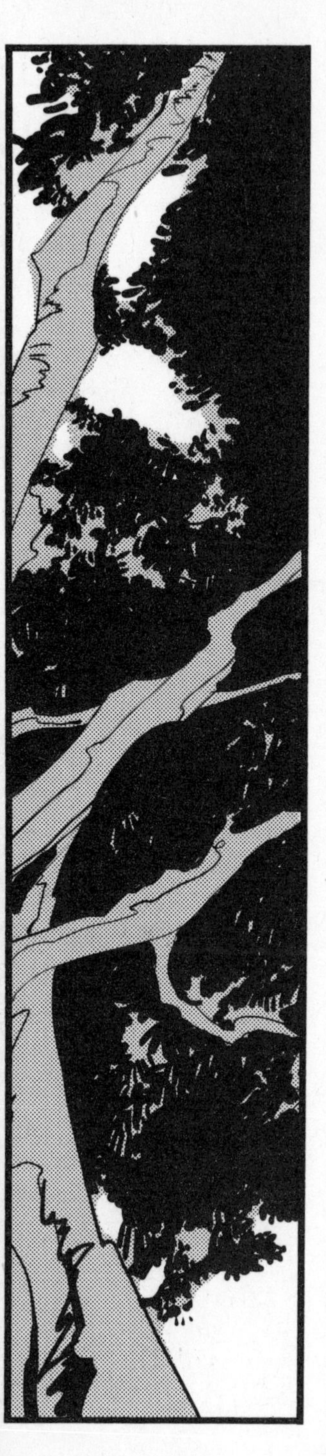

ARE YOU NOT ATTENDING THE MEETING?
...MM.

IT SEEMS OTUS IS SPEAKING DIRECTLY WITH CHIEF OFFICER LILIUM.

...SO IT SEEMS.

SIR...
ARE YOU ALL RIGHT?

...MM.

CHAPTER 35

The Night Before, the Weight of True Intent in Badon

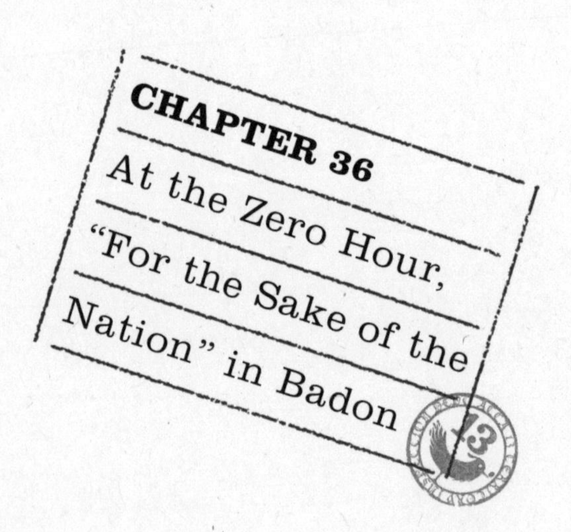
CHAPTER 36
At the Zero Hour,
"For the Sake of the
Nation" in Badon
13

TOMORROW ...
IT WILL BE SUNNY IN BADON, YES?
QUALM...

YES.
THAT IS THE FORECAST.
MM.

I SUPPOSE SCHWAN'S LEFT?
YES.

IT'S A TERRIBLE THING FOR HIM...
...BUT IT CAN'T BE HELPED.
...I AM TRULY SORRY...
...THAT WE CAN PROTECT THE COUNTRY NO OTHER WAY.
IT'S NOT YOUR FAULT, QUALM.
IT'S BECAUSE I AND MY DAUGHTERS SPOILED THAT BOY.

YOU REALLY HAVE DONE EXCELLENT WORK FOR THE HOUSE OF DOWA.
I WAS SURPRISED WHEN YOU CURBED THE CIGARETTE INDUSTRY AND RAISED TAXES IN CONSIDERATION OF THE STRESS ON ME WHEN I STOPPED SMOKING FOR MY HEALTH.
BUT THANKS TO THAT, I'VE MANAGED TO LIVE A LONG LIFE.

AND THEN PRINCESS SCHNEE'S SON BECOMES SUCH A DEVOTED SMOKER...
IT'S QUITE IRONIC.

THE BOY TAKES AFTER ME.

I ALSO MUST THANK YOU FOR WHAT YOU DID FOR SCHNEE...
...AND FOR ALLOWING ME TO SEE HER CHILDREN.
I AM SINCERELY GRATEFUL.

YOU'LL SEE THEM AGAIN...
...HERE, IN THIS ROOM IN DOWA...

...IN JUST
A LITTLE
WHILE.

IT WAS CHIEF OFFICER GROSSULAR'S JOB TO GO OVER THE PLAN TONIGHT, BUT SINCE HE'S NOT FEELING WELL...
...I, LILIUM, WILL TAKE ON THE TASK OF BRINGING YOU UP TO DATE.

THIS IS OUR LAST MEETING BEFORE EXECUTING THE PLAN.
I'D LIKE TO GO OVER TOMORROW'S SCHEDULE...
...ONE LAST TIME.

PRINCE JEAN IS ALSO HERE WITH US TODAY.

ACCA
NOW, THEN.
THE FATE OF ACCA AND THE THIRTEEN DISTRICTS RESTS ON THIS COUP.
WE CANNOT CHANGE THE PLAN NOW.

WE COULD CANCEL IT.
BUT AS WE ARE ALL OF THE SAME MIND, I ASSUME NO ONE WISHES TO DO SO?

NOW, THE FINAL CHECK.

ACCA BADON
THE RIOT SQUAD OF THE BADON BRANCH POLICE WILL BE THE ENFORCERS.
YOU PATROL OFFICERS ARE ON CROWD CONTROL...
...IN CASE OF UNREST AMONG THE CITIZENS WHO HAVE COME TO WATCH OR WHO ARE VIEWING THE BROADCAST.

SO WE'RE REALLY DOING THIS, HUH?
THE COUP...
I THINK IT'LL HAPPEN.
I MEAN, WE SERIOUSLY OUTNUMBER THE PRINCE.
WITH THE COUNCIL AND THE ROYAL GUARD, WE'RE TALKING FIFTEEN PEOPLE MAX.
AND THEY'RE ALL PRETTY BOYS, TO BOOT.
THE WAY I HEARD IT JUST NOW, THE PRIVY COUNCIL...
...KNOWS ABOUT THE COUP, AND THEY'RE THROWING THE PRINCE UNDER THE BUS.

SOUNDS LIKE IT'S A TOTAL GO, AM I RIGHT?
....

SO WHO'S THE NEXT KING IF THE PRINCE IS OVER-THROWN?
WHAT'LL WE DO IF HE SAYS HE'S GETTING RID OF ACCA?
RIGHT?
SHUT UP, YOU GUYS!

SO WHEN ARE THEY GOING TO ANNOUNCE THAT THE OTUSES ARE ROYALTY...?
...I WONDER IF LOTTA'S OKAY.
I'LL PROTECT HER FROM THE REPORTERS WHO SWARM HER!

THE NEW CAKE...
...IS YUMMYYYY!

I'M SO GLAAAAD!
THE NUTS GIVE IT THIS GREAT CRUNCH!
I'LL BUY SOME TO TAKE HOME TO MY BROTHER!
THANKS, CHAIR-MAN...
...FOR INVITING ME.
...JEAN TOLD ME...
...YOU PROBABLY ALREADY KNOW.
ABOUT OUR FAMILY...

AFTER THE CEREMONY TOMORROW...
...EVERYONE IN THE DEPARTMENT IS HAVING DINNER. WOULD YOU LIKE TO JOIN US?
ARE YOU SURE?
OF COURSE.
BUT IT MIGHT BE A BIT MORE LIVELY THAN USUAL...
THERE'LL BE THIRTEEN MORE OF US.

MAY I...

...SAY SOME-THING?

WHEN WE SEIZE THE PRINCE AND HIS PEOPLE...
...WE'RE GOING TO MAKE HIM SWEAR ON THE SPOT TO YIELD HIS RIGHT TO INHERIT.
BUT PERHAPS WE COULD DO THAT AT A LATER DATE?

RATHER...
...I THINK IT'S BEST I DON'T STAND ON CENTER STAGE TOMORROW.
THINGS WILL GO MUCH MORE SMOOTHLY IF WE TRY TO AVOID HURTING THE PRINCE'S FEELINGS.

I THINK HE'LL GET OBSTINATE IF I'M THERE.

HE JUST MIGHT.
HEH HEH.
WE ARE TALKING ABOUT THE PRINCE, AFTER ALL.

SO...
...I'LL LEAVE THE CONVERSATION WITH HIM TO YOU CHIEF OFFICERS.
PLEASE MAKE MY BEING A ROYAL PUBLIC LATER...
...AFTER YOU'VE GOTTEN THE PRINCE'S WRITTEN VOW.
WELL, THEN...
...IS THIS ACCEPTABLE TO EVERYONE?

IT SHOULD...
...EXPEDITE MATTERS.

IF YOU NEED SOMETHING, THEN COME CLOSER.

...I'M SMOKING, THOUGH.

I DON'T MIND.

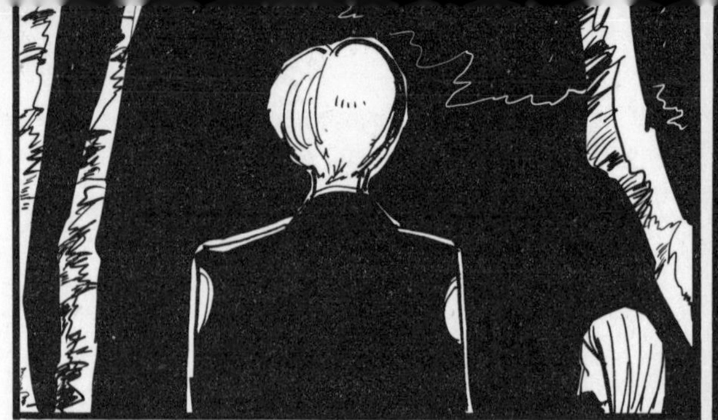

TOMORROW'S TIMETABLE, HM?

YOU'RE ALL RIGHT WITH THIS?

...THERE'S NOTHING FOR YOU TO BE UPSET ABOUT, CHIEF OFFICER GROSSULAR.
PLEASE DON'T LOOK AT ME LIKE THAT.

WHAT DO YOU BELIEVE IS THE NUMBER ONE THING TO DO FOR THE SAKE OF THIS COUNTRY?

CAN I TAKE A LITTLE OF YOUR TIME?
I'VE BEEN WANTING TO SPEAK WITH YOU, CHIEF OFFICER.

ABOUT THIS NATION...

...AND ACCA...

...WE COULD TALK...
...UNTIL MORNING AND STILL HAVE MORE TO SAY.

THERE ARE NO PROBLEMS HERE.
THE PRINCE IS SULKING A LITTLE, BUT YOU REAP WHAT YOU SOW.
You're harsh with your master, Magie.
AS I SAID, YOU REAP WHAT YOU SOW.

BUT...
...I DO WONDER IF THE ROYAL GUARD DOESN'T NUMBER TOO FEW ...?

The prince didn't want more.
He said there was no need to go all-out for something like ACCA.
......
The Privy Council chair also did not suggest extra person-nel.

EXCUSE ME.
ARE YOU LACKING FOR ANYTHING?
EVERY-THING!
......
...WEREN'T YOU GOING TO MAKE ME EAT SANDWICH BREAD?
I WON'T FORCE YOU.
DID YOU WISH TO?
FORGET IT!
TOMORROW WILL BE A BUSY DAY. PLEASE GET A GOOD NIGHT'S REST.
I WILL EXCUSE MYSELF FOR TODAY, THEN.
PATAN (SHUT)
....
....

IT REALLY IS DIFFERENT, ISN'T IT?
I'VE FELT A TENSION IN THE AIR IN TOWN SINCE THIS MORNING.

And how are you?
ME?
WERE YOU WORRIED?
I'M PERFECTLY FINE.
IT SEEMS MISS LOTTA'S GOING TO THE PLAZA WITH FRIENDS TO WATCH THE ACCA CENTENNIAL CEREMONY.
SO I CAN AT LEAST WATCH OVER HER FROM WITHIN THE CROWD.
I EXPECT JEAN'LL BE ALL RIGHT.
HE'S UNDER THE PROTECTION OF ACCA.

STILL, THAT'S ONLY PHYSICALLY...
...BUT I'M NOT ESPECIALLY WORRIED.

I WONDER WHY.
MAYBE BECAUSE IT'S JEAN.

ALL RIGHT.
IT'S TIME.
MM.

WHERE'S YOUR BROTHER, LOTTA?
SOME-WHERE IN THE MIDDLE, I THINK. WE PROBABLY WON'T BE ABLE TO SEE HIM.

...HUH?
JEAN'S ALL THE WAY UP THERE...
BUT EVERYONE ELSE IS AN ACCA BIG SHOT...
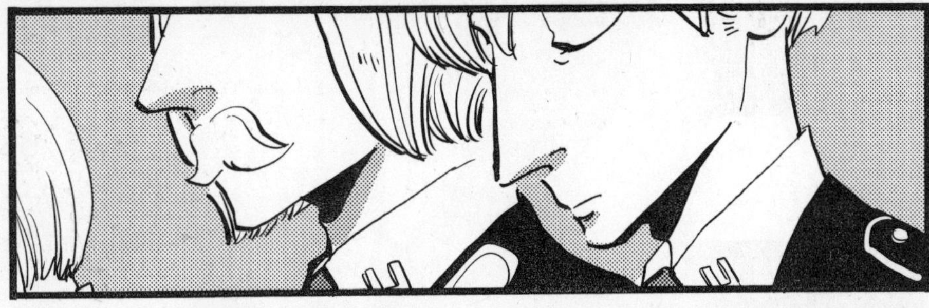

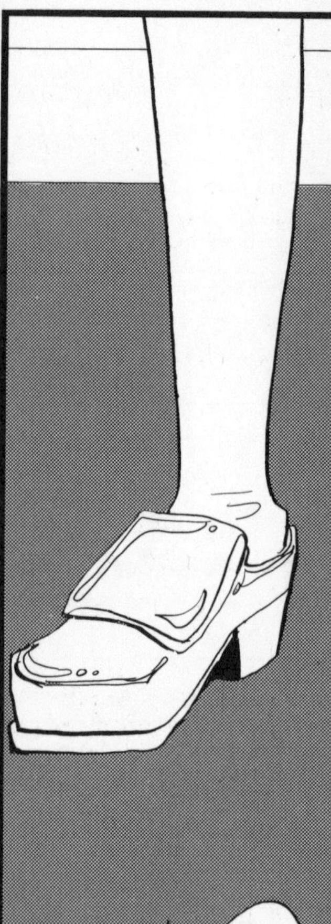

KO
(TAK)

IT'S THE PRINCE.
THAT'S PRINCE SCHWAN.
SO HE'S THE NEXT KING?

SO, HOW DOES THIS GO?
AFTER THE NATIONAL AND ACCA ANTHEMS...
...THERE WILL BE A GREETING FROM THE ACCA CHIEF OFFICERS AND THE DIRECTOR GENERAL.
THEN YOUR SPEECH.
AND THEN—
I DON'T CARE.
ACCA

...THE ONLY ONES HERE...
...WHO DON'T KNOW ABOUT THE COUP...
...ARE THE PRINCE AND HIS PEOPLE...
...AND THE AUDIENCE...

ACCA

ACCA
13

WHAT IS THE MEANING OF THIS?
A COUP D'ÉTAT? PUTTING THE ENTIRE COUNTRY IN DANGER?
AND LED BY ACCA, WHO NEVER SHUT UP ABOUT "PROTECTING THE COUNTRY"!?
...IT'S TO PROTECT THE COUNTRY.
カッ
KA' (TAK)

WE WOULD PROTECT THAT VERY ACCA FROM THE HEIR...
...WHO INTENDS TO ELIMINATE IT.
IT'S NOT ONLY US.

THERE IS NOT A SINGLE PERSON...
...WHO WISHES YOU TO INHERIT THE CROWN...
...NOT EVEN IN THE HOUSE OF DOWA.
...WHAT? A COUP?
HE SAID HE WAS GONNA GET RID OF ACCA? THAT'D BE BAD.
BUT ACCA'S THE REASON WE HAVE PEACE.
THE COUNTRY'LL GRIND TO A HALT WITHOUT ACCA.

SO IS THE PRINCE SAYING HE LIKES WAR?
HE'S TOTALLY DIFFERENT FROM HIS MAJESTY.
HE'S NOT THINKING ABOUT THE COUNTRY.
SOMEONE LIKE THAT BECOMES KING, WE'RE ALL IN TROUBLE.
IT'S OBVIOUS THERE'LL BE WAR AGAIN.
NO PRINCE SCHWAN!

NO!
NO!
...SO YOU'RE OVERTHROWING ME HERE...
...AND PROPPING SOMEONE ELSE UP AS KING, THEN.
SOMEONE WHO WILL PROTECT ACCA.

WHY ARE YOU JUST STANDING THERE?
ACCA 13

WHY DON'T YOU COME FORWARD?

CHAPTER 36

At the Zero Hour, "For the Sake of the Nation" in Badon

FINAL CHAPTER

The Day the Bird of ACCA Spreads Its Wings

JEAN...

YOU ARE THE ONLY PRINCE IN THIS COUNTRY RIGHT NOW...
...PRINCE SCHWAN.

PLEASE REFRAIN FROM SPEAKING IN CONJECTURES. YOU WILL THROW THE PEOPLE NTO DISARRAY.

13
ACCA PROTECTS THIS NATION.

THAT'S THE SAME AS PROTECTING THE DOWA ROYAL FAMILY, THE SYMBOL OF THIS COUNTRY.

THIS NATION HAS DEVELOPED AND PROSPERED UNDER THE DOWA REIGN.
THE DOWA FAMILY IS A SYMBOL OF PEACE.
DOWA

THE CONTINUED PEACE OF THE HOUSE OF DOWA...
...MEANS THE PEACE OF THIS LAND.
THIS WAS NOT IN THE SCHEDULE, WAS IT?

YOU ARE THE SUCCESSOR TO THE HOUSE OF DOWA.
WE WOULD LIKE YOU TO TAKE GREATER CARE OF YOURSELF.
THE FACT THAT YOU TRUST ACCA...
...ENOUGH TO ATTEND WITH JUST A FEW GUARDS...
ザッ
ZA (FSH)

...IS A GREAT HONOR FOR US AT ACCA.
BUT, WELL... ALL THINGS IN MODERATION.

I AM AWARE THAT THE MEMBERS OF THE ROYAL GUARD ARE A SELECT ELITE.

BUT CONSIDERING YOUR POSITION IS SUCH THAT THE BARREL OF A GUN MIGHT BE TURNED ON YOU AT ANY TIME, AS WE DEMONSTRATED NOW...
...WE WOULD ASK THAT THEY ALWAYS BE PERFECTLY PREPARED.

WE WISHED TO TAKE THIS OPPORTUNITY TO REMIND YOU OF THIS...
...AND SO WE INCORPORATED THIS PIECE OF THEATER INTO THE CEREMONY.
PLEASE FORGIVE OUR INSOLENCE.

BUT YOUR HIGHNESS'S CONSIDERATION IN NOT MAKING A SHOW OF POWER...
...HAS NO DOUBT ALSO IMPRESSED THE PEOPLE.

THE DOWA BLOODLINE DOES NOT LOVE WAR.
AND SO THERE IS PEACE.

PEACE WILL NOT COME TO A LAND UNDER A RULER WHO FLAUNTS THEIR STRENGTH.

ACCA WILL PROTECT THIS COUNTRY UNDER THE RULE OF THE HOUSE OF DOWA.

WE ENTRUST YOU WITH THE FUTURE OF ACCA, PRINCE SCHWAN.

...I SHOULD LIKE...

...ACCA TO...
...PROTECT THIS COUNTRY FOR ALL TIME.

WAAH!
NINO ...?
YOUR HIGHNESS.
YOUR HAND.
WAAAH!
THANK YOU VERY MUCH.
WAAAH!
....

WAAAH!
THIS...
......
WAS IT JUST US FROM FURAWAU...
WAAAH!
...WHO WERE NOT INFORMED OF THIS FARCE...?

WAAAH!

IF YOU'RE GOING TO TAKE RISKY GAMBLES...
...YOU HAVE TO KEEP THE PETTY TRICKS TO A MINIMUM.
I WONDER IF FURAWAU STILL INTENDS TO CONTINUE THE GAME?

...YOU TOO?

IT WAS YOU, THEN?

WHEN DIRECTOR GENERAL MAUVE TOLD ME I WAS ROYALTY IN KORORE...
...WE DECIDED ON A STRATEGY FOR TODAY.

WE MADE FURAWAU'S GAME ACCA'S GAME...
...AND NOW WE'VE WON.

"VICTORY" FOR FURAWAU IS DIFFERENT FROM "VICTORY" FOR ACCA.
IF ACCA WINS, THEN FURAWAU'S GAME ENDS THERE TOO.
ACCA
13
ACCA'S "WIN" IS TO ENSURE THE CONTINUANCE OF ACCA.
THE DISMANTLING OF ACCA WOULD CAUSE THE DISTRICTS TO FEAR THE COLLAPSE OF SELF-GOVERNANCE, AND FURAWAU WAS GOING TO TAKE ADVANTAGE OF THAT SENSE OF CRISIS...
...TO TRY TO STAND IN FOR DOWA IN THE END...
IN WHICH CASE, ACCA HAD TO GO AWAY FOR YOU TO TAKE CONTROL.

SO SPECULATION, THEN?
NO, THAT'S NOT IT, IS IT?

DIRECTOR GENERAL MAUVE INVESTIGATED FURAWAU'S INTERNAL ADMINISTRATION.

APPARENTLY, SHE GOT TESTIMONY FROM...
...THE FURAWAU REPRESENTATIVE TO THE CENTRAL COUNCIL.

...SO WE CAN'T ACTUALLY TRUST ANYONE OUTSIDE HOUSE LILIUM.

...WHAT WILL YOU DO?
WILL YOU CHANGE YOUR STRATEGY AND CONTINUE THE GAME?

FURAWAU WILL STEP AWAY...

...FROM THIS GAME OF THE KINGDOM OF DOWA.

YOU MADE THIS HAPPEN...
...DIRECTOR GENERAL MAUVE.

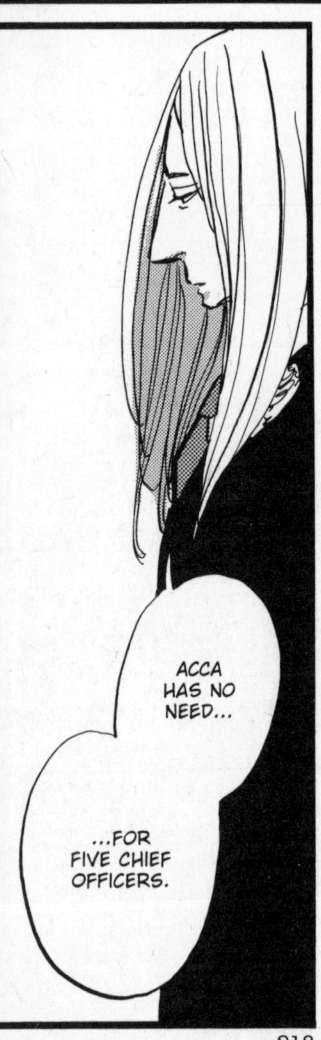
ACCA HAS NO NEED...
...FOR FIVE CHIEF OFFICERS.

ACCA 13
THE FIVE LEADERS WHO WERE CENTRAL TO THE FOUNDING OF ACCA A HUNDRED YEARS AGO SIMPLY WENT ON TO BECOME ITS CHIEF OFFICERS.
WE'RE NOTHING BUT A VESTIGE.

I SUGGEST WE ELIMINATE THE POSITION OF CHIEF OFFICER.

AGREED.
NO OBJECTIONS.
MM.

YOU'RE THE CHIEF.
LAST NIGHT...
...AFTER OTUS TOLD ME EVERYTHING...
...I HESITATED TO EVEN STAND HERE TODAY AS ONE OF THE CHIEF OFFICERS.

I SEE NOW...
...THAT THE THIRTEEN UNIFORMS OF ACCA...
...ARE A SYMBOL OF UNITY.
ACCA
13

THANK YOU.

JEAN.
AGENT RAIL LET ME IN.
REALLY?
THAT WAS QUITE THE CEREMONY, HUH?
NINO WAS BY MY SIDE...
...BUT HE WAS GONE BEFORE I KNEW IT...

YOUR HIGHNESS, ARE YOU SURE YOU DON'T WISH TO SAY SOMETHING?
...NO NEED.
YOU DON'T HAVE TO BE SHY.

UM...
THANK YOU...
...FOR LETTING ME KNOW MY LIFE WAS IN DANGER BEFORE.
IT WAS MY DOING.
....
...THANK THAT ONE IF YOU MUST.
PUI (SNUB)
YOU GAVE MAGIE THE ORDER, THOUGH, RIGHT, YOUR HIGHNESS?
HE DID.
HE WAS QUITE CONCERNED ABOUT BOTH OF YOU.
....
....
THE TWO OF YOU MAY COME TO THE CASTLE IN DOWA.

IT WOULD PLEASE GRAND-FATHER!

THEY DIDN'T EVEN REVEAL THE VICE-CHAIRMAN AS A ROYAL.
THAT WAS MAGNIFICENT.
...DON'T TELL ANYONE ELSE, LOCUSTELLA.
I KNOW.

NOW, THEN.
ALTHOUGH EVERYTHING'S SETTLED, I'M SURE TENSION WILL LINGER AT EACH BRANCH BECAUSE OF THIS INCIDENT.
YOU MUST ALL FOCUS AND TAKE CARE OF THAT.

THE INSPECTION DEPARTMENT WILL RETURN TO OUR ORIGINAL, CRUCIAL ROLE.
TO INSPECT EACH DISTRICT, OF COURSE.

I'LL BE HANDING OUT YOUR NEXT POSTS AT THE DINNER PARTY TONIGHT.
I HAVE THEM ALL IN HERE.
EEP!
I'M SO NERVOUS!
WHAT'S THIS ENVELOPE?
THE USUAL TRANSFER REQUEST FROM JEAN.
TRANSFER REQUEST

ACCA
HELLO, EVERYONE!
WELCOME TO OUR TOUR OF ACCA!
ACCA

ACCA
THIS IS OUR FIRST TOUR SINCE ACCA WAS RESTRUCTURED.
ACCA
Headquarters
Tour
09:30-11:30
14:00-16:00
I WONDER IF ANY OF YOU CAN TELL ME WHAT'S CHANGED?

THERE ARE TWELVE DISTRICTS NOW INSTEAD OF THIRTEEN.
ACCA 13
SO WHY DIDN'T THE NUMBER IN THE ACCA SYMBOL CHANGE?

THE CHIEF OFFICER SYSTEM CHANGED...
...AND THE PERSON AT THE VERY TOP OF ACCA IS NOW THE DIRECTOR GENERAL.
CHIEF OFFICER HAS BEEN MADE AN HONORARY, CONSULTING POSITION.
YES! YOU OVER THERE!
THERE USED TO BE FIVE IMPORTANT PEOPLE, AND NOW THERE'S ONE!
THAT'S RIGHT!

I HAVE A QUESTION!
AND WHAT'S THAT?

IT WAS THE CHIEF OFFICERS' ONLY REQUEST.
I HAD NO OBJECTIONS.
ACCA Director General Mauve

SO YOU INITIALLY INTENDED TO ELIMINATE THE CHIEF OFFICER POSITION?

THE DIRECTOR GENERAL WISHED US TO STAY ON AS ADVISORS.
I ACCEPTED HER DIRECT APPOINTMENT.
ACCA Chief Officer Grossular

AND THE REASON WHY THE ACCA SYMBOL IS UNCHANGED?

I HOPE FURAWAU WILL SOMEDAY...
...RETURN TO THE KINGDOM OF DOWA.
13

Following Furawau's independence, there was some concern over our nation's natural assets.
But the outlook has changed dramatically with the discovery of underground resources in Pranetta.
PRANETTA

IT'S A MIRACLE.
BHK
THIS MAKES PRANETTA THE WEALTHIEST DISTRICT IN THE COUNTRY NOW.
THESE RESOURCES DON'T BELONG TO PRANETTA ALONE.
THEY BELONG TO THE KINGDOM OF DOWA.
HAVE SOME LEMONADE!
The number of young people moving to Pranetta to chase their dreams only continues to grow.
YAKKARA
The number making the move from Yakkara is particularly remarkable.

BIT MORE ROOM TO BREATHE IN YAKKARA NOW. ALL'S WELL THAT ENDS WELL, HM?
I'M RETIRED, THOUGH. ACCA, THE GOVERNMENT... NONE OF MY CONCERN ANYMORE.
AND IF YOU DON'T MIND, I'M IN THE MIDDLE OF A POKER GAME.
Former ACCA Chief Officer Spade

WE'VE MADE FURTHER IMPROVEMENTS AND SUCCEEDED IN PRODUCING AN EVEN LARGER STRAWBERRY.
MY FIRST JOB SINCE BECOMING THE GOVERNOR OF JUMOKU? WELL...
IT'S TO OPEN BOUTIQUES IN EVERY DISTRICT.
I WANT TO EXPAND THE REACH OF JUMOKU SPECIALTIES.
Jumoku District Governor Pine
I'D LOVE IT IF WE COULD OPEN ONE UP IN SUITSU AT SOME POINT TOO.
YOU'LL SOON BE SELECTING THE COUNCIL REPRESEN-TATIVE.
BUT WHAT LED TO THE FIRST GENERAL ELECTION IN SUITSU...
...DISTRICT GOVERNOR PASTIS?
TAKE A LOOK. DON'T YOU THINK THE VIEW IS LOVELY?
THE BEAUTY OF OUR SUITSU NEVER CHANGES.
Suitsu District Governor Pastis

I NEVER DREAMED...
...YOU'D BE ENDORSED AS A CANDIDATE FOR THE COUNCIL.
BEURRE
BEURRE
ALL THE CITIZENS LOVE SUITSU.
IT'S UNTHINKABLE THAT THE PERSON SELECTED BY THOSE CITIZENS TO BE OUR REPRESENTATIVE COULD DO ANYTHING TO SULLY THIS BEAUTY.
THIS WILL MAKE OUR DISTRICT EVEN MORE BEAUTIFUL.

SUITSU IS CHANGING.
BISC

FROM A "COUNTRY" TO A "DISTRICT."

HACHIKUMA ...
...ROLL CAKE!

THANKS, EIDER!
LET'S EAT!
LET'S EAAAT!
HOW'VE YOU BEEN?
IT'S ALREADY TWO MONTHS SINCE YOU QUIT ACCA?
AND QUITTING TO GET MAAAAR-RIED!!
RIIIGHT ...!?
...BUT IT WAS ONLY GOOD FOR A FEW DAYS BEFORE THE NEW POSTING.
YOU'RE HAVING SOME TOO, RIGHT, KNOT?
UH-HUH.
KATA (CLACK)
KATA
I MEAN, PESHI IS JUST TOO FAR AWAY!
THE FORMER SUPER VISOR'S...
...FISH ARE EVERY-WHERE...
I SUPPOSE AGENT GRUS IS FISHING RIGHT ABOUT NOW.
YOU SHOULD'VE GONE TOO, EIDER. TO PESHI...
I THOUGHT I WOULD TALK TO THE CHAIRMAN ABOUT THAT...
HE'S OFF TODAY.
THIS ALWAYS HAPPENS TO YOU, HUH, EIDER?

PI (BEEP)
ピ
ピ PI
Trans-mission from Yakkara.
Hello there.
AGENT CANARII!
HELLO.
WE'VE FINISHED THE SYSTEM UPGRADE. COULD YOU PLEASE CONFIRM ON YOUR END?
Agent Canarii! How's Yakkara?
You having fun?
You're not bank-rupt?
YOU MEAN FROM GAM-BLING?
I'M NOT VERY GOOD AT THAT.

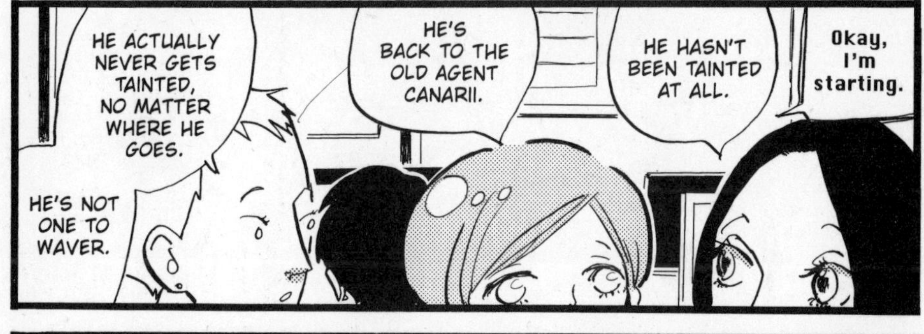
Okay, I'm starting.
HE HASN'T BEEN TAINTED AT ALL.
HE'S BACK TO THE OLD AGENT CANARII.
HE ACTUALLY NEVER GETS TAINTED, NO MATTER WHERE HE GOES.
HE'S NOT ONE TO WAVER.

AND EVEN A GUY LIKE HIM WAS CHANGED BY FURAWAU.
I GUESS IT'S A PRETTY FRIGHTENING PLACE.

WHERE DID THE INFORMATION THAT JEAN OTUS WAS OF ROYAL BLOOD...
...LEAK FROM IN THE END, THEN?

PERHAPS SOMEONE WANTED TO ELIMINATE...
...ANY OBSTACLE TO THE CONTINUATION OF THE DOWA FAMILY LINE?

WELL, IT DOESN'T MATTER NOW, HM?
IT'S GOT NOTHING TO DO WITH HOUSE LILIUM...

...OR THE COUNTRY OF FURAWAU.

THINGS WENT OFF ALMOST TOO MUCH TO PLAN.
I SCARE EVEN MYSELF.

YOUR HIGHNESS.
MUGIMAKI
MISS LOTTA HAS COME FROM BADON.

YOU'RE ALONE THIS TIME?
YES.
HERE. I BROUGHT SANDWICH BREAD.
...I'LL ACCEPT IT.

THIS IS FROM AGENT RAIL FOR YOU, MAGIE.
GIVE THIS TO MAGIE...
AND THAT ONE?
THIS IS FOR THE FIRST PRINCESS...
...TO THANK HER FOR TELLING ME ABOUT MY MOTHER LAST TIME...
...SHE'S THE VERY PERSON WHO TRIED TO HAVE YOU KILLED.

BUT...SHE APOLOGIZED AND ALL.
AND SHE'S MY MOTHER'S SISTER.

...GRANDFATHER IS WAITING.
PREPARE SOME SNOWBALLS.

MISS LOTTA HAD APPLE CAKE AT THE DOWA "SNOWBALL" SHOP...
...AND REALIZED IT TASTES EXACTLY THE SAME AS MR. BAUM'S APPLE CAKE IN BADON.
THE FLAVOR HAS BEEN PASSED DOWN IN THEIR FAMILY FOR GENERA-TIONS.
I LOVE THAT CAKE MYSELF.
THEY'VE DONE GOOD WORK FOR US.

THAT WAS QUITE IMPRESSIVE.

ALL ON THE INSTRUCTIONS OF PRIVY CHAIR QUALM.

A CLEAN SWEEP OF THE LILIUM FAMILY AND THEIR SCHEMES WAS NECESSARY...
...BEFORE PRINCE SCHWAN SUCCEEDED THE THRONE.
TO ELIMINATE FUTURE GRIEF...

THE INVOLVEMENT OF THE OTUSES...
WELL, I DIDN'T ANTICIPATE THAT EITHER.

YOU WERE THE ONE WHO PUSHED THE PRIVY CHAIR AFTERWARD, WEREN'T YOU?
YOU SAID THERE WAS NO WAY JEAN WOULD WANT THE THRONE ONCE HE FOUND OUT ABOUT HIS ORIGINS.
YOU'VE HAD HIM MOVING ACCORDING TO YOUR PLANS FOR THE LAST SIX MONTHS. YOU HAD TO HAVE KNOWN.

IT WASN'T QUITE A GAMBLE.
YOU SHOULD KNOW THAT BETTER THAN ANYONE.
YES.

...WE'VE HAD THE CHANCE TO SPEAK DIRECTLY BEFORE...
...BUT THIS IS THE FIRST TIME YOU'VE ASKED TO MEET.

THE KING NO LONGER NEEDS PHOTOS.

YOU ARE RELEASED FROM THAT ROLE.

YOU'RE FREE.
LIVE AS YOU PLEASE.

IT'S TIME.
I HAVE TO GO.

I'LL DO JUST THAT.

GOOD-BYE.
I'M SURE WE'LL MEET AGAIN.
I'LL BE THE SAME AS ALWAYS.

AND YOU'LL BE LIVING YOUR OWN LIFE.
BATAN (SLAM)
バタン
WHERE TO?
BEAK SALON IN THE EAST SECTOR. ...COULD YOU PERHAPS HURRY?
I THINK I'M GOING TO BE LATE FOR MY APPOINTMENT.

DYEING MY HAIR BLOND IS SUCH A BOTHER.

TRANSFER REQUEST

びりっ
BIRI (RIP)
TRANSFER REQUEST
TRANSFER REQUEST FROM JEAN OTUS?
WHAT ARE YOU TALKING ABOUT?
I'VE NEVER SEEN SUCH A THING.

CAFE

Inspection Department
VICE-CHAIRMAN.
YOU MUST BE TIRED AFTER YOUR TRIP.
NOT ESPECIALLY, TO BE HONEST.
...
MY SCHEDULE THIS TERM'S PRETTY RELAXED.
LAST TERM WAS SO HECTIC TOO.
THIRTEEN DISTRICTS IN SIX MONTHS...
THE CHAIRMAN REALLY STRUGGLED TO PUT THAT PLAN TOGETHER.
IS COFFEE ALL RIGHT?
IT'S THE BLEND FROM THE CAFÉ DOWNSTAIRS.
MM.
THEY'RE ALWAYS HAVING COFFEE AT THAT CAFÉ, HM?
DIRECTOR GENERAL MAUVE AND CHIEF OFFICER GROSSULAR ...

DON'T YOU THINK THEY LOOK GOOD TOGETHER?
I DO!
IT'S LOVELY, ISN'T IT?
VICE-CHAIRMAN...
LOTTA'S AWAY RIGHT NOW, ISN'T SHE?
HOW ARE YOU FOR DINNER?
DID YOU WANT ALL OF US TO GO OUT?
OH, KELI!
MAYBE HE'S GOING OUT WITH HIS GIRL-FRIEND?
OH RIGHT!
KACHI (CHIK)
ガチ
...DOES HE HAVE A GIRLFRIEND?

...I LOST MY PARENTS IN THE PESHI-ROKKUSU TRAIN ACCIDENT.

MY MOTHER WORKED AS A VOLUNTEER...
...AND SOMETIMES, SHE WOULD GO VISIT THE DIFFERENT DISTRICTS.
THAT TIME, MY FATHER WAS WITH HER.
I MET CHIEF OFFICER GROSSULAR WHEN HE WAS VISITING THE FAMILIES OF THE DECEASED WITH THE ROKKUSU DISTRICT GOVERNOR.
HE PUT HIS HAND ON MY SHOULDER...
...AND HE JUST STARED AT ME. DIDN'T SAY A WORD.
IF IT'S TRUE MY MOTHER WAS ROYALTY...
...I THINK MAYBE THE CHIEF OFFICER KNEW THEN.
MAYBE HE SAW SOME KIND OF MOVEMENT IN THE DOWA ROYAL FAMILY.

...SO YOU'RE SAYING CHIEF OFFICER GROSSULAR WAS THE ONE WHO REVEALED YOUR LINEAGE...?
HE WOULDN'T DO THAT.
NO.
NOT THAT...
...I THINK THAT'S THE KIND OF PERSON CHIEF OFFICER GROSSULAR IS.
...YOU REALLY ADMIRE HIM...
...THE CHIEF OFFICER...
I GOT INTERESTED IN ACCA BECAUSE OF HOW PROUD CHIEF OFFICER GROSSULAR WAS OF IT.
AND THEN SOMEONE WITH THE SAME WILL AS HIM SHOWED UP...
...AND TOOK THE POSITION OF ACCA DIRECTOR GENERAL.

I KNOW MY FEELINGS ARE UNREQUITED.
YOU'RE THE SAME WAY.
I ALSO HAVE NOTHING BUT RESPECT FOR THE CHIEF OFFICER.

ACCA MUST NOT BE DISBANDED.
THAT'S RIGHT.

WE'RE GOING TO A HARE BUFFET TONIGHT.
WHY DON'T YOU COME WITH US?
I'M FINE FOR FOOD.

AND IF I GO HAVE A DRINK BY MYSELF...
...MY PARTNER IN CRIME'LL SHOW UP.

HERE.
HM?

...THERE'S SOME FOR ME TOO?

IT WAS SUPPOSED TO BE FOR KNOT, BUT HE LEFT EARLY.
WHAT'S WRONG WITH KNOT?
HE GOT A PHONE CALL.
FROM HIS WIFE!
SHE SAID SHE WAS AT THE BADON AIRPORT.
KNOT WENT TO PICK HER UP.

IT'S PERFECT THAT WE HAD ONE EXTRA.
YOU'RE LUCKY, VICE-CHAIRMAN!

RIIIIGHT?
WELL, OF COURSE.

I MEAN, THE VICE-CHAIRMAN WALKS AROUND WITH THAT ACCA LIGHTER...
...WHICH IS BASICALLY LIKE WALKING AROUND WITH GOOD LUCK IN YOUR POCKET.

ACCA 13-TERRITORY INSPECTION DEPARTMENT 6 END

FINAL CHAPTER

The Day the Bird of ACCA Spreads Its Wings

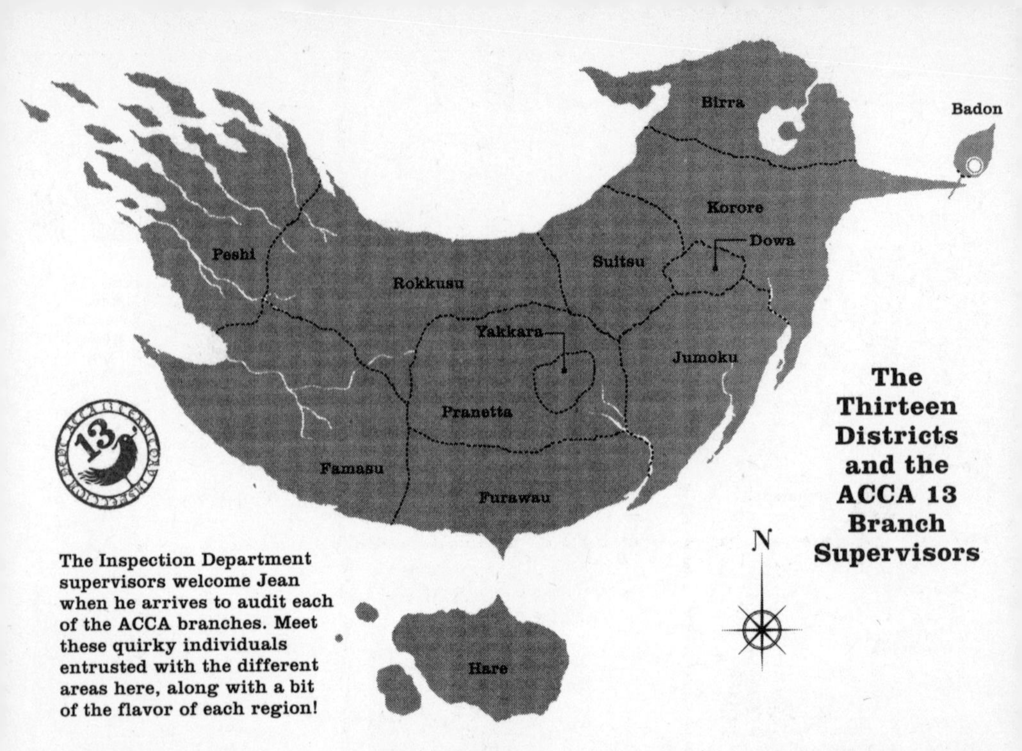

The Thirteen Districts and the ACCA 13 Branch Supervisors

The Inspection Department supervisors welcome Jean when he arrives to audit each of the ACCA branches. Meet these quirky individuals entrusted with the different areas here, along with a bit of the flavor of each region!

Information is tightly controlled here to preserve the culture of the district. People from outside are restricted even in where they can eat, and the ACCA agents stationed here are no exception to this rule.

Suitsu Supervisor **Warbler**

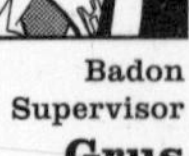

ACCA headquarters is also in the capital city of Badon, and the branch office is right next door. The food at the branch office cafeteria is said to be delicious.

Badon Supervisor **Grus**

Hare Supervisor **Parus**

The climate in this district is comfortable, and the people are all long-lived. The secret to a long life is a healthy diet and a peaceful smile.

All kinds of things in this district are a little on the large side. Especially appealing is the food, and staff are obsessed with the popular fast-food joint Basswood. There's not a supervisor who doesn't gain weight during their posting here.

Jumoku Supervisor **Koruri**

Korore Supervisor
Larus

In this wonderful district, old and stylish buildings line the streets, where the women cut a dashing figure as they walk along. The chocolate is incredible.

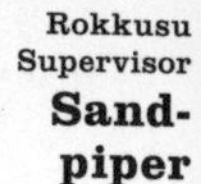

Rokkusu Supervisor
Sand-piper

In this rough, rocky town, many of the men are slender with long hair, which goes well with the traditional dress.

Birra Supervisor
Dunlin

In this cold district where it's always snowing, cold-weather gear is a must. Or warming up with a stiff drink...

Dowa Supervisor
Egret

Dowa is a key district and home to the royal family, as well as a number of traditional sweets. Under the patronage of the royal family, the people cultivate a strong aesthetic sense, and the supervisors also take care with their appearance.

Famasu Supervisor
Eider

The large farms of this district produce 90 percent of the country's agricultural product. The freshly picked produce is all delicious.

Furawau Supervisor
Canarii

With its wealth of natural resources, this is a affluent district, its towns enveloped in the scent of flowers.

Pranetta Supervisor
Locustella

Because the land is a desert, life is actually lived underground in this district. It's inconvenient in some ways, such as poor reception and the heat below the surface, but the faces of the citizens are sunny.

Peshi Supervisor
Passer

The district is surrounded by water, and birds can be found everywhere. Since it's easy to catch a lot of fish, most of the agents stationed here fish as a hobby.

Yakkara Supervisor
Falco

Gamblers come together in this district with the hope of getting rich quick. Even the smallest things are decided with cards.

ACCA
13

Translation:
Jocelyne Allen

Lettering:
Lys Blakeslee

Yen Press
1290 Avenue of the Americas
New York, NY 10104

Visit us at yenpress.com
facebook.com/yenpress
twitter.com/yenpress
yenpress.tumblr.com
instagram.com/yenpress

First Yen Press Edition: February 2019

Yen Press is an imprint of Yen Press, LLC.
The Yen Press name and logo are trademarks of Yen Press, LLC.

The publisher is not responsible for websites (or their content) that are not owned by the publisher.

Library of Congress Control Number: 2017949545

ISBNs: 978-1-9753-8277-3 (paperback)
978-1-9753-8278-0 (ebook)

10 9 8 7 6 5 4 3 2 1

WOR

Printed in the United States of America